AF505016

The Truth about Dragons

Michael Pennington
The Truth about Dragons

All rights reserved
Copyright © 2024 by Michael Pennington

No part of this publication may be reproduced, distributed, or transmitted in any form or by any means, including photocopying, recording, or other electronic or mechanical methods, without the prior written permission of the publisher, except in the case of brief quotations embodied in critical reviews and certain other noncommercial uses permitted by copyright law.

—

Published by - Spines
ISBN: 979-8-89569-986-7

The Truth about Dragons

Michael Pennington

Introduction

Jessica and Michael enter the antique store, the weathered floorboards protesting beneath their feet. A symphony of creaks and groans greets them as if the store itself is whispering secrets of a forgotten era. The musty scent of old books and ancient relics invades their nostrils, a perfume both alluring and unsettling.

We wander through the labyrinth of shelves, our eyes drinking in the eccentric assemblage of artifacts: porcelain dolls with vacant stares, rusted swords that once tasted blood, and faded maps promising paths to nowhere. Each item seems to carry the weight of untold stories, tales that dance just beyond the edges of my comprehension.

As we venture deeper into the store's shadowy recesses, a peculiar sensation prickles at the base of my skull. It's as if an unseen presence is watching us, its gaze as heavy as the dust that coats every surface. I glance at Michael, searching for a flicker of unease in his eyes, but his expression remains inscrutable.

Do you feel that? I whisper, my voice barely rising above the oppressive silence.

He nods, his brow furrowing. It's as if the air is alive with something... something ancient and powerful.

In the dimly lit corner, a weathered tome catches my eye. Its leather binding is cracked and peeling, and the pages are yellowed with age. An inexplicable force draws me toward it as if the book itself is calling out to me.

We approach the tome with cautious steps, our heartbeats quickening in unison. The air grows thick with an unspoken anticipation, a sense that we are teetering on the precipice of a dark revelation.

My fingers tremble as they hover above the book's surface, hesitating to make contact. What secrets lie within its pages? What forgotten knowledge awaits, ready to unravel the fabric of our reality?

The decision hangs in the balance, a choice between blissful ignorance and the siren's call of forbidden wisdom. At that moment, I realize that our fate has already been sealed. The book has chosen us, and there is no turning back from the path it has laid before our feet.

With a deep breath, I let my fingers brush against the weathered spine and a jolt of energy courses through my veins. It's a sensation both exhilarating and terrifying, a whisper of ancient power that resonates deep within my soul.

Michael's gaze meets mine, a silent understanding passing between us. We are kindred spirits at this moment, bound by a shared curiosity that overrides our instinctual fear.

Together, we carefully open the book, its hinges creaking with the weight of centuries. The pages are filled with faded ink and intricate symbols, their meanings lost to time. As we stare at the cryptic text, the air around us seems to grow heavy, as if the very essence of the room is being drawn into the book's pages.

"What do you think it means?" Michael murmurs, his voice barely audible above the thundering of my own heartbeat.

I shake my head, unable to tear my eyes away from the mesmerizing patterns. "I don't know, but I can feel it... like a presence watching us from the shadows."

The symbols seem to dance before my eyes, their edges blurring and shifting in the flickering candlelight. A sense of vertigo washes over me, and for a moment, I feel as though I am falling into the pages, my consciousness slipping away from the confines of my mortal body.

Michael's hand on my shoulder anchors me back to reality, his touch a lifeline in the midst of the swirling darkness. "We shouldn't linger here," he whispers urgently. "There's something about this book... something that feels wrong."

But even as he speaks, I find myself drawn deeper into the arcane symbols, their secrets whispering to me from across the ages. The weight of forgotten knowledge presses down upon us, and I know that we have stumbled upon something far greater and more terrible than we could have ever imagined.

The air grows thick with an unnatural stillness as if time itself has been suspended within the pages of the ancient tome. At that moment, I realize that our fates have become inexorably entwined with the secrets that lie within, and there is no turning back from the path that has been laid before us.

As the ancient words consume my thoughts, I feel a strange sensation creeping up my spine, like icy fingers trailing along my skin. The room seems to fade away, replaced by a void of swirling shadows and distant whispers that beckon me deeper into the mysteries of the text.

"Jessica?" Michael's voice sounds distant, muffled by the pounding of my own heart. "Are you alright?"

I try to respond, but my tongue feels heavy, as if weighted down by the secrets I have absorbed. The symbols on the page blur and shift, rearranging themselves into patterns that dance at the edge of comprehension.

Time loses its meaning as we delve further into the cryptic passages, our minds consumed by the tantalizing glimpses of forbidden knowledge. The outside world fades away, replaced by a realm of ancient wisdom and dark secrets that threaten to unravel the very fabric of our reality.

In the depths of my mind, I hear a voice whispering, its tone seductive and alluring. "Embrace the power," it murmurs, "and all the secrets of the universe shall be yours."

I feel myself slipping away, drawn into the voice's promise of endless knowledge and power. But even as I teeter on the brink of surrender, a small part of me clings desperately to the remnants of my sanity, fighting against the insidious pull of the ancient text.

"We have to stop," I manage to whisper, my voice hoarse and strained. "This knowledge... it's too much. It will consume us."

Michael's grip on my shoulder tightens his presence, a fleeting anchor in the midst of the gathering darkness. "We've come too far to turn back now," he says, his eyes gleaming with a feverish intensity. "We must see this through to the end, no matter the cost."

And so, we press on, our minds consumed by the secrets that dance just beyond our grasp. With each passing moment, I feel the weight of the ancient knowledge settling upon my soul, its dark tendrils burrowing deep into the recesses of my being.

In the flickering candlelight, the shadows seem to lengthen, reaching out to embrace us in their cold, ethereal grasp. As we descend further into the depths of the ancient text, I cannot help but wonder if we have sealed our own fate, forever bound to the secrets that now possess our very souls.

The candle sputters, its flame dancing erratically as if sensing the growing unease that permeates the room. I watch, transfixed, as the shadows on the walls twist and morph into grotesque shapes, their edges sharpening with each flicker of light.

"Do you feel that?" I whisper, my voice trembling. "It's like the very air is alive with something... something ancient and malevolent."

Michael nods, his face pale in the dimming light. "The book... it's awakening something. Something that should have remained dormant."

As if in response to his words, a sudden gust of wind sweeps through the room, extinguishing the candle with a hiss. Darkness engulfs us, thick and suffocating, and I feel my heart pounding against my ribcage.

"Michael?" I call out, my voice sounding small and distant in the oppressive silence.

But before he can respond, a surge of dark energy erupts from the book, filling the room with a palpable sense of dread. It washes over us in waves, cold and insidious, seeping into our very bones.

I gasp, my body convulsing as the energy courses through me, its touch like icy tendrils wrapping around my heart. Beside me, Michael staggers, his eyes wide with a mixture of fear and realization.

"What have we done?" he whispers, his voice barely audible above the pounding of my own heartbeat.

And in that moment, as the darkness swirls around us, I know that our actions have set something in motion. Something that cannot be undone. The ancient forces we have unleashed now threaten to consume us, body and soul.

With trembling hands, I reach for Michael, seeking comfort in his presence. But even as our fingers intertwine, I feel the weight of our transgression bearing down upon us, a suffocating burden that threatens to crush us beneath its immense power.

In the suffocating darkness, I close my eyes, desperately seeking a glimmer of hope amidst the encroaching shadows. But all I find is the echo of our own folly, a haunting reminder of the price we must now pay for our insatiable curiosity.

And so, we sit in the darkness, our minds reeling from the realization of our own hubris. The ancient text lies before us, its secrets now a curse rather than a blessing. As the night deepens around us, I cannot help but wonder if we will ever find our way back to the light or if we are forever doomed to wander in the shadows of our own making.

The ethereal figure's words hang heavy in the air, a portentous warning that chills me to the bone. I can feel the weight of

Michael's gaze upon me, a silent question lingering between us: What have we done?

"You must find the strength within yourselves," the figure whispers, its voice a haunting melody that echoes through the room. "The path ahead is fraught with peril, but it is the only way to restore the balance you have disturbed."

I swallowed hard, and my throat suddenly dried. "How?" I manage to croak out, my voice trembling with a mixture of fear and desperation.

The figure seems to shimmer, its form shifting like mist in the wind. "Seek the Ethereal Realm of the Dragons," it intones, its words carrying a power that resonates deep within my soul. "There, you will find the answers you seek and the allies you need to face the darkness that now threatens to consume all."

Michael's hand tightens around mine, a silent reminder that we are in this together. I draw strength from his presence, even as the enormity of our task threatens to overwhelm me.

"But be warned," the figure continues, its voice growing more urgent. "The forces you have unleashed will stop at nothing to prevent you from succeeding. You must be prepared to face your deepest fears and darkest secrets, for they will be your greatest enemies on this journey."

I nod, my jaw clenched with determination. I know that the road ahead will be long and treacherous, but I also know that we have no choice but to follow it. The fate of the world now rests upon our shoulders, a burden that we must bear, no matter the cost.

As the figure begins to fade, its form dissolving into the shadows, I feel a sudden surge of energy coursing through my veins. It is as if the ancient magic of the text has awakened something within me, a power that I never knew I possessed.

And with that power comes a glimmer of hope, a faint light in the darkness that threatens to consume us. I know that the journey ahead will be filled with danger and uncertainty, but I also know that we must press on, no matter what horrors lie in wait.

For the sake of the world, and for the sake of our own souls, we must find the strength to face the darkness and to emerge victorious on the other side. And so, with a heavy heart and a determined spirit, we set forth into the unknown, ready to face whatever challenges may come our way.

I turn to Michael, my voice trembling with a mixture of fear and resolve. "We have to close the book," I whisper, my eyes flickering toward the ancient tome that lies open before us. "We have to seal away the darkness that we've unleashed."

Michael nods, his face grim. He reaches out with shaking hands, his fingers hovering over the weathered pages. I can see the hesitation in his eyes, the fear that even this simple act might somehow make things worse.

But we both know that we have no choice. We have to act before it's too late.

Together, we grasp the edges of the book, our knuckles turning white with the force of our grip. And then, with a swift, decisive motion, we slam it shut, the sound echoing through the room like a thunderclap.

For a moment, nothing happens. The air is still, the silence deafening. But then, slowly, I begin to feel a change. The darkness that had been pressing in on us began to recede, the shadows growing shorter and less menacing.

And yet, even as the immediate danger fades, I know that our troubles are far from over. We have awakened something ancient and powerful, something that will stop at nothing to consume the world in darkness.

We have to find a way to stop it. We have to seek out the knowledge and power that we need to combat this rising threat. And we have to do it quickly before it's too late.

I meet Michael's gaze, my eyes burning with fierce determination. "We have to do this," I say, my voice low and intense. "We have to find a way to fix what we've done."

He nods, his expression mirroring my own. "Whatever it takes," he says, his words a solemn vow. "We'll do whatever it takes to make this right."

And with those words, we set forth on a journey that will test the very limits of our strength and courage. A journey that will take us to the darkest corners of the world and the darkest depths of our own souls.

But we have no choice. The fate of the world depends on us, and we will not fail.

The door to our home creaks open, a plaintive cry that echoes through the stillness. Inside, the air is heavy with the weight of our discovery, the ancient text clutched tightly in my trembling hands.

"We need to study this further," Michael says, his voice a distant echo in the tumult of my thoughts. "There must be answers hidden within its pages."

I nod, my mind already racing with the possibilities. What secrets does this text hold? What dark powers have we unleashed upon the world?

We set to work, clearing a space amidst the clutter of our lives. Books and papers are pushed aside, replaced by the tools of our newfound quest. Pens and notebooks, reference materials and ancient tomes were all scattered across the surface of our makeshift study.

Time loses all meaning as we pore over the pages, our eyes straining in the flickering candlelight. The symbols dance before us, their meanings tantalizingly close yet always just out of reach.

"There must be a pattern," I mutter, my fingers tracing the lines of faded ink. "Some kind of code that we're missing."

Michael leans in closer, his brow furrowed in concentration. "Maybe it's not just the words themselves," he says slowly. "Maybe it's the way they're arranged, the spaces between them."

We work in silence, the only sound of the scratching of our pens and the rustle of turning pages. The hours slip by the world outside, fading away until there is only this room, this text, and the weight of our responsibility.

And yet, even as we search for answers, I can feel the darkness pressing in around us. The shadows seem to lengthen, the air growing colder with each passing moment. It's as if the house itself knows what we've done and is slowly turning against us.

"We have to hurry," I whisper, my voice barely audible over the pounding of my heart. "We're running out of time."

Michael looks up, his eyes meeting mine in the flickering light. "We'll find a way," he says, his voice steady and sure. "We have to."

And so we press on, our minds and hearts consumed by the task at hand. The fate of the world hangs in the balance, and we are the only ones who can set things right.

But even as we work, I can't shake the feeling that we're being watched, that something dark and ancient is lurking just beyond the edges of our vision, waiting for the perfect moment to strike.

And I know, with a terrible certainty, that our journey has only just begun.

The candle gutters cast frenzied shadows across the walls as we pore over the ancient text. The symbols seem to swim before my eyes, their meaning tantalizingly close yet slipping through my grasp like wisps of smoke. Michael's brow furrows in concentration, his fingers tracing the faded ink as if he could divine its secrets through touch alone.

"There must be something we're missing," he mutters, frustration seeping into his voice. "A key to unlocking this cipher."

I nod, my own mind racing with possibilities. The weight of our discovery presses down upon me, a physical burden that settles in my bones. The knowledge we seek feels like a double-edged sword, promising power and understanding, but at what cost?

As the night wears on, the air in the room grows heavy and stale, thick with the dust of forgotten tomes and the tang of our own sweat. The silence is broken only by the frantic scratching of pens and the rustle of turning pages. Time loses all meaning as we delve deeper into the mysteries before us.

But even as we search for answers, I can feel a creeping unease settling over me. It's as if the shadows in the corners of the room are growing longer, reaching out with tendrils of darkness to ensnare us. The floorboards creak with a sinister rhythm, and the walls seem to pulse with a malevolent energy.

I try to shake off these unsettling thoughts, telling myself that it's just my imagination running wild. But deep down, I know that we've unleashed something far beyond our understanding. The ancient text whispers to me in the silence, its words a siren song that threatens to lure us into madness.

"We're close," Michael says, his voice cutting through my reverie. "I can feel it."

I look up at him, seeing the determination etched into the lines of his face in that moment, I know that we will stop at nothing to unravel the truth, no matter the price we may pay.

As we continue our study, the room becomes a sanctuary of knowledge and determination. The candle's flame flickers, casting long shadows on the walls, as Jessica and Michael delve further into the mysteries of the ancient transcription. But even as we press forward, I can't shake the feeling that we're being watched by something ancient and malevolent, biding its time until we make one fatal mistake.

Chapter 1

Inciting Incident

The ancient text lay open before us, its yellowed pages whispering secrets in an arcane tongue. I traced my finger along the delicate symbols, feeling a strange electricity tingle beneath my skin.

"Jessica, look at this passage," Michael said, his eyes gleaming with excitement. "It almost seems to shimmer when I touch it."

I leaned closer, my breath catching as the intricate glyphs appeared to writhe and dance. "Be careful," I warned, a chill creeping up my spine. "We don't know what power lies dormant in these words."

But even as I spoke, my own fingertips betrayed me, drawn inexorably to the enigmatic script. The apartment faded away, replaced by visions of starry realms and spectral dragons. Had I known then the horrors we would unleash, would I have stayed my hand?

Michael's voice cut through my reverie. "Do you feel that? It's like the air is... vibrating."

I nodded, unable to tear my gaze from the text. "We should stop," I whispered, though I made no move to close the book. "This is dangerous."

"Or it could be the key to everything," Michael argued, his

expression fever bright. "Think of the knowledge we could uncover!"

As we continued to study the arcane symbols, a part of me screamed to run, to burn the cursed tome and forget we'd ever seen it. But a darker voice whispered of power beyond imagination, of mysteries long forgotten by mortal minds.

"Just a little longer," I murmured, more to myself than to Michael. "We're so close to understanding..."

Little did we know, with each caress of those eldritch runes, we drew closer to our doom - and the doom of countless innocents. The weight of that sin would haunt me for eternity.

A sudden surge of energy erupted from the pages, dark and malevolent. The room shuddered, books tumbling from shelves as an unseen force pressed down upon us. The air grew thick and oppressive as if we had been plunged into the depths of some cosmic abyss.

"Jessica," Michael gasped, his face ashen. "What have we done?"

I met his gaze, my heart hammering against my ribs. The terror in his eyes mirrored my own, a silent acknowledgment of the catastrophe we had unwittingly set in motion.

"I don't know," I whispered, my voice barely audible over the low, ominous thrumming that filled the air. "But something's terribly wrong."

The ancient text before us seemed to pulse with an unholy light, the symbols we'd so carelessly traced now writhing on the page like living things. I wanted to look away, to flee, but found myself paralyzed by a mixture of fear and morbid fascination.

"We need to close it," Michael said, reaching for the book with trembling hands. "Maybe if we—"

His words were cut short as another wave of energy rippled outward, knocking us both back in our chairs. The walls of our once-cozy apartment seemed to warp and twist, reality itself bending under the strain of whatever eldritch forces we had awakened.

"It's too late," I murmured, a cold certainty settling in my gut. "We've opened a door that was never meant to be opened."

As the room continued to quake around us, I couldn't help but wonder: what price would we – and the world – pay for our insatiable curiosity?

I stumbled to the window, drawn by an unseen force. My breath caught in my throat as I gazed upon the city I once knew. New York had become a nightmarish hellscape, its towering skyline now a twisted mockery of itself.

"Michael," I choked out, "you need to see this."

He joined me, his face ashen. "Dear God," he whispered.

Shadows writhed across buildings like living ink, their tendrils reaching hungrily toward the ground. The air itself seemed to whisper, a cacophony of voices speaking in tongues long forgotten.

"What have we done?" I asked, though I knew he had no answer.

The floor beneath us shuddered violently. Cracks spider-webbed across the pavement below, glowing with an unholy light. As we watched, horrified, clawed hands burst forth from the fissures.

"They're coming through," Michael said, his voice tight with panic. "We've opened a gateway."

I couldn't tear my eyes away from the demonic forces clawing their way into our world. A part of me wondered if this was retribution for past sins, for the darkness we had both carried within us.

"We need to leave," I said, finally finding my voice. "Now."

But even as the words left my lips, I knew there was nowhere to run. The nightmare we'd unleashed was spreading, and we were at its epicenter.

My legs felt like lead as I stumbled away from the window, my heart pounding so hard I thought it might burst from my chest. Michael's hand found mine, his grip tight and trembling.

"The book," I gasped, my eyes darting to the ancient text still lying open on our dining table. "We can't leave it."

We scrambled toward it, our movements frantic and uncoordinated. As my fingers closed around its worn leather cover, a jolt of energy surged through me, and I nearly dropped it.

"Jessica," Michael's voice was strained, "we need to go. Now."

I clutched the book to my chest, its weight both comforting and terrifying. "Where?" I asked, my voice barely a whisper. "Where can we possibly go?"

Michael's eyes met mine, and I saw my own fear reflected in them. "Anywhere but here," he replied.

We stumbled toward the door, the floor beneath us groaning and shifting. The walls seemed to pulse with otherworldly energy, shadows dancing across them in a macabre waltz.

"This is our fault," I choked out as we reached the hallway. "We should have known better than to meddle with things we didn't understand."

Michael's grip on my hand tightened. "We'll fix this," he said, but I could hear the doubt in his voice.

As we fled down the stairs, the building itself seemed to cry out in agony. The air grew thicker with each step, filled with whispers that clawed at the edges of my sanity.

"Do you think we can truly undo this?" I asked, my breath coming in ragged gasps.

Michael didn't answer immediately, and in that silence, I heard the weight of our guilt, the crushing burden of the consequences we now faced.

"We have to try," he finally said as we burst out onto the street. "We're the only ones who can."

The world outside had transformed into a nightmarish hellscape. Shadows writhed across crumbling facades, their tendrils reaching out to snatch at fleeing figures. The air was thick with ash and the acrid stench of brimstone.

"Oh God," I whispered, clutching the ancient text even tighter. "What have we done?"

Michael's face was ashen as he surveyed the chaos. "We need to move," he said, his voice barely audible above the cacophony of screams and shattering glass.

We darted down the street, dodging falling debris and the grasping hands of shadowy entities. My heart pounded in my chest, each beat a reminder of our culpability.

"Look out!" Michael shouted, pulling me back as a car careened past, its driver's face a mask of terror.

I stumbled, my eyes drawn to a nearby building as it collapsed in on itself. The screams from within would haunt me forever.

"Those people," I choked out. "We... we killed them."

Michael's grip on my arm tightened. "We didn't mean for this to happen," he said, but the words rang hollow.

We pressed on, weaving through the pandemonium. Each step felt like a betrayal; each breath was stolen from those we'd condemned.

"How could we have been so foolish?" I asked more of myself than to Michael. "So arrogant to think we could control such power?"

He didn't answer, and I knew he was grappling with the same crushing guilt. We had unleashed this horror upon the world, and now we were running from it like cowards.

We stumbled into a narrow alley, our lungs burning as we gasped for air. The stench of decay and brimstone clung to my nostrils, a constant reminder of the hell we'd unleashed. I pressed my back against the cold brick wall, my legs trembling beneath me.

"Jessica," Michael panted, his eyes wild with fear and something else—determination, perhaps? "We can't keep running. We have to face this."

I laughed, a bitter sound that echoed off the alley walls. "Face it? How? We're not heroes, Michael. We're the villains in this story."

He grabbed my shoulders, forcing me to meet his gaze. "No. We made a mistake, but we can fix it. We have to."

I wanted to believe him, but the weight of our sins pressed down on me, threatening to crush what little hope remained. "And if we can't?"

"Then we die trying," he said, his voice barely a whisper.

I closed my eyes, memories of the chaos we'd caused flashing behind my lids. The screams, the destruction, the lives torn apart—all because of us. When I opened them again, I saw the same resolve in Michael's eyes that I felt stirring in my chest.

"Okay," I said, my voice steadier than I felt. "Where do we start?"

As if in answer, an unearthly howl echoed through the alley, sending shivers down my spine. We were out of time, out of options. There was only one path forward, and it led straight into the heart of the nightmare we'd created.

"We go back," Michael said, gripping my hand tightly. "Back to where it all began."

I nodded, steeling myself for what lay ahead. We had opened Pandora's box, and now we had to find a way to close it—or die in the attempt.

I clutched the ancient text to my chest, my fingers trembling as they traced the intricate symbols etched into its weathered cover. Its weight seemed to increase with each passing second, as if the very fate of the world was pressing down upon us.

"Jessica," Michael's voice cut through my spiraling thoughts, "look at this."

He pointed to a passage I hadn't noticed before, his hazel eyes wide with a mix of fear and fascination. As I leaned in, the words seemed to shimmer and dance on the page, revealing their terrible truth.

"The dragons," I whispered, my voice barely audible over the distant screams. "They're real. And we... we can summon them."

Michael's jaw clenched. "It's our only hope. But at what cost?"

I laughed, a hollow sound that echoed in the alley. "Cost? Look around us, Michael. What more do we have to lose?"

He didn't answer, but I saw the weight of our decision settle on his broad shoulders. We both knew there was no turning back now.

"Let's go," I said, pushing myself to my feet. "Before I lose what little courage I have left."

We stepped out of the alley, the chaos of the city washing over us like a tidal wave. Buildings crumbled in the distance, demonic shrieks pierced the air, and the acrid smell of smoke and brimstone filled my lungs.

As we navigated the treacherous streets, I couldn't shake the feeling that we were walking to our doom. But what choice did we have? We'd unleashed this hell, and now we had to find a way to end it—or die trying.

The streets grew darker, shadows elongating into monstrous shapes that seemed to reach for us with hungry claws. I clutched the ancient text to my chest, its leather binding slick with my sweat.

"Jessica," Michael whispered, his voice tight with tension. "Look there."

I followed his gaze to a group huddled in the ruins of what was once a bustling café. Their eyes, wide and haunted, locked onto us with a desperation that made my skin crawl.

"Please," a woman with matted grey hair croaked, her trembling hand outstretched. "Help us."

I hesitated, torn between our mission and the raw need before us. "We can't," I muttered, more to myself than to them. "We have to keep moving."

But as I turned away, a man's anguished cry pierced my resolve. "You did this, didn't you? I can see it in your eyes!"

His accusation hit me like a physical blow. I stumbled, my grip on the text faltering. Michael caught my arm, steadying me.

"We're trying to fix it," he said, his voice carrying a strength I wished I felt. "We're going to make this right."

A bitter laugh rang out from the group. "How? By running away?"

I closed my eyes, fighting back tears. "We're not running," I said, my voice barely above a whisper. "We're seeking... something that can help. Something powerful."

The despair in their faces flickered, giving way to a fragile hope. It was almost worse than their accusations.

"Come with us," I heard myself say, even as my mind screamed at its foolishness. "We can't promise safety, but..."

"But it's better than waiting here to die," Michael finished, his eyes meeting mine with a mix of approval and worry.

As the survivors rose on shaky legs, I wondered if I'd just sealed their fate along with ours. The weight of the text seemed to grow heavier with each step we took into the encroaching darkness.

Chapter 2

Call to Action

I stared at the ancient parchment spread before us, my eyes wide and unblinking. The dim light from the single lamp cast eerie shadows across the yellowed text, making the inked symbols seem to writhe and pulse with a life of their own. Beside me, Jessica's breath came in short, ragged gasps.

"What have we done?" Her voice was barely a whisper, trembling with the weight of our terrible realization.

I couldn't bring myself to answer. My feet moved of their own accord, pacing back and forth across our small apartment. Each step felt like trudging through thick mud, my limbs leaden with dread.

Jessica's fingers clutched the edges of the parchment, her knuckles white. "Michael, I think... I think we've awakened something. Something beyond our control."

Her words sent icy tendrils of fear creeping up my spine. I ran a hand through my hair, tugging at the roots as if the pain might wake me from this nightmare. But I knew there would be no waking; this was all too real.

"We couldn't have known," I muttered, more to myself than to her. "How could we have possibly known?"

But even as the words left my lips, I knew they rang hollow.

We should have known better than to meddle with forces beyond our comprehension. The crushing weight of guilt pressed down upon me, threatening to suffocate me.

Jessica's eyes met mine, filled with a terror that mirrored my own. "What do we do now?"

I wish I had an answer for her. My mind raced, grasping desperately for some solution, some way to undo what we had set in motion. But every possibility seemed more hopeless than the last.

"I don't know," I admitted, my voice hoarse. "God help me, Jessica, I don't know."

The silence that followed was deafening, broken only by the frantic pounding of my heart. I paced the room, each step echoing the rhythm of my racing thoughts. Suddenly, a wild idea struck me.

"Magic," I blurted out, turning to face Jessica. "We need to fight fire with fire."

Her brow furrowed. "What do you mean?"

"The dragons," I said, the words tumbling out faster than I could process them. "Those legendary creatures from the ancient texts. If we could summon them..."

Jessica's eyes widened. "Are you mad? We've already meddled with forces beyond our understanding. And now you want to—"

"Do you have a better idea?" I snapped, immediately regretting my tone. "I'm sorry, I just... we have to do something."

She nodded slowly, her face a mask of reluctant acceptance. "Where do we even start?"

I grabbed my laptop, fingers flying over the keys. "We research. We dig. We don't stop until we find a way."

Hours blurred together as we scoured every resource we could find: dusty tomes from forgotten libraries and obscure online forums filled with cryptic ramblings. My eyes burned from the endless scrolling, and my fingers were stained with ink from hastily scribbled notes.

Our small apartment transformed into a chaotic nexus of

magical inquiry. Books and papers littered every surface, forming treacherous towers that threatened to topple at the slightest touch. The air grew thick with the musty scent of ancient knowledge and our own growing desperation.

"Michael," Jessica's voice cut through my concentration. "Look at this."

I peered over her shoulder at a faded manuscript, its edges crumbling beneath her trembling fingers. The words seemed to writhe on the page as if trying to escape our prying eyes. A chill ran down my spine as I read the passage, each word carving itself into my mind with terrifying clarity.

"This can't be real," I whispered, but deep down, I knew it was. We had stumbled upon something far greater and more terrible than we could have ever imagined. And now, there was no turning back.

My heart pounded as Jessica's trembling voice filled the room, each word dripping with a weight I couldn't fathom. "The dragons, ancient guardians of Earth, slumbered beneath celestial veils, their scales forged from starlight and cosmic fire."

The words seemed to pulse with an otherworldly energy, clawing at the edges of my sanity. I couldn't shake the feeling that we'd stumbled upon a truth never meant for mortal eyes.

"Keep reading," I urged my voice barely a whisper.

Jessica continued, her words painting a haunting picture of beings beyond comprehension. "They alone stood between our world and the encroaching darkness, their very breath holding reality together."

A cold dread settled in my gut. What had we awakened? What cosmic balance had we disturbed?

"Michael," Jessica's voice cracked, her eyes wild with a mix of fear and desperate hope. "If this is true, if the dragons really existed..."

I seized on the thought, a manic energy coursing through me. "Then they're our only hope," I finished, the words tasting of ash and salvation. "We have to find a way to summon them, Jess. It's the only way to fix what we've done."

The weight of our task pressed down on me, threatening to crush my resolve. But beneath the fear, a spark of determination ignited. We had unleashed this darkness upon the world. Now, we would do whatever it took to make it right.

"How?" Jessica whispered, her doubt mirroring my own unspoken fears.

I met her gaze, steeling myself against the madness that threatened to consume us both. "We keep searching. We don't stop until we find a way to reach the Ethereal Realm. Whatever it takes."

The air in our cluttered apartment grew heavy with the weight of our decision. As we turned back to our frantic research, I couldn't shake the feeling that we were hurtling toward a fate beyond our understanding, guided by the ghostly whispers of long-forgotten cosmic guardians.

I hunched over the coffee table, its surface a chaotic sea of papers and open books. My hand trembled as I scrawled another potential lead onto our growing list. Jessica sat cross-legged on the floor, her hair a tangled mess, chewing absently on the end of her pen.

"The Whispering Caves," I muttered, my voice hoarse from hours of discussion. "Legends say they echo with dragon song."

Jessica's eyes, once bright with curiosity, now dulled by exhaustion, met mine. "And the Crystal Spires of Avalon? They're said to pierce the veil between worlds."

I nodded, adding it to our list. Each possibility seemed more far-fetched than the last, yet we clung to them like drowning men to driftwood.

"Michael," Jessica's voice wavered, barely above a whisper. "What if... what if we can't do this? What if we're just two fools stumbling in the dark?"

The doubt in her words mirrored the fear gnawing at my own heart. I reached out, grasping her hand. It was cold, trembling slightly beneath my touch.

"We have to try," I said, forcing conviction into my voice. "The alternative is... unthinkable."

But even as I spoke, images of the chaos we'd unleashed flashed through my mind. What horrors had we set loose upon the world? And who were we to think we could undo it?

Jessica's fingers tightened around mine, drawing strength from our shared desperation. "You're right," she whispered, a flicker of determination rekindling in her eyes. "We started this. We have to finish it."

I nodded, pushing aside the doubts that threatened to paralyze us. We were walking a razor's edge between salvation and damnation. But we would walk it together into whatever dark future awaited us.

I rose, my bones aching from hours hunched over arcane texts. "We need to leave," I said, the words tasting of ash and regret. "There are whispers of those who still practice the old ways. Perhaps they can guide us."

Jessica's eyes met mine, a maelstrom of fear and resolve swirling in their depths. "Where do we even begin?"

I grabbed our coats, the weight of our mission settling upon my shoulders like a funeral shroud. "The underground," I muttered, my voice barely audible. "Where secrets fester and magic still breathes."

We stepped out into the night, the city's neon glow casting sickly shadows across our faces. The streets pulsed with life, oblivious to the darkness we'd unleashed. How many of these souls would be consumed by our folly?

"Stay close," I whispered to Jessica, gripping her hand as we plunged into the churning sea of humanity. Faces blurred past, each a reminder of what we stood to lose. The air felt thick and oppressive as if the very atmosphere sensed the coming storm.

We wove through alleyways, our steps quickening with each passing moment. The weight of our transgression drove us forward, a relentless taskmaster spurring us on.

"Michael," Jessica's voice cut through the cacophony of the city. "Do you truly believe we can fix this?"

I paused, the lie catching in my throat. "We must," I finally replied, the words hollow even to my own ears. "For if we cannot, then we are damned indeed."

As we pressed on, the city's façade seemed to peel away, revealing glimpses of a world hidden beneath – symbols etched in doorways, figures lurking in shadows. We were stepping into a realm where reality bent, and nightmares took form.

And all the while, the darkness we'd awakened loomed behind us, patient and hungry, waiting for the moment when our strength would fail.

The hidden library loomed before us, a decrepit monolith of crumbling stone and twisted iron. Its very presence seemed to warp the air around it, a mirage of forbidden knowledge.

"This is it," I murmured, my voice barely a whisper. "Our last hope."

Jessica's grip tightened on my arm. "Michael, I'm... I'm afraid."

I couldn't bring myself to reassure her. The truth was, I was terrified, too.

We pushed open the ancient doors, their hinges groaning like tortured souls. The musty air within assaulted our senses, thick with the scent of decaying parchment and secrets long buried.

"Hello?" Jessica called out, her voice echoing unnaturally in the cavernous space.

Silence answered, broken only by the skittering of unseen creatures in the shadows.

"We shouldn't be here," I thought, even as we ventured deeper into the gloom. Towering shelves loomed on either side, their contents hidden beneath layers of dust and time.

A flicker of movement caught my eye. "There," I hissed, pointing to a hooded figure gliding between the stacks.

"Excuse me," Jessica called out, her voice trembling. "We need help."

The figure turned; its face hidden in the depths of its cowl. When it spoke, the voice was neither male nor female but a whisper that seemed to come from everywhere at once.

"You seek that which should remain hidden," it said, the words slithering into my mind. "Why do you disturb the slumber of ancient powers?"

I swallowed hard, fighting the urge to flee. "We... we made a mistake. We need to make it right."

A dry chuckle, like rustling leaves. "Mortals always seek to undo their folly. But some bells cannot be unrung."

"Please," Jessica pleaded. "There must be a way."

The figure was silent for a long moment. I could feel its gaze upon us, weighing our souls.

"Perhaps," it finally said. "But the price may be more than you're willing to pay."

"Anything," I said, desperation clawing at my throat. "We'll do anything."

Another chuckle, this one tinged with something that might have been pity. "Seek the Enigmatic Seer. In the realm where starlight dances on crystal peaks. Only she can guide you now."

With that, the figure seemed to melt into the shadows, leaving us alone with our dread and a fragile sliver of hope.

We stumbled out of the library, the cool night air a shock against my feverish skin. Jessica's hand found mine, her fingers trembling.

"Michael," she whispered, her voice barely audible above the distant hum of the city. "Do you think... do you think we can really find her?"

I squeezed her hand, trying to steady us both. "We have to. The Enigmatic Seer is our only hope now."

We exchanged a glance, determination burning in Jessica's eyes. I wondered if she could see the fear lurking behind mine.

"Where do we even start?" she asked.

"I don't know," I admitted, my mind racing. "But 'the realm

where starlight dances on crystal peaks'... it has to mean something."

We set off down the darkened street, our footsteps echoing hollowly. The city seemed different now as if it were holding its breath. Shadows stretched longer and darker, reaching for us with grasping fingers.

"Do you feel that?" Jessica murmured, huddling closer to me.

I nodded, unable to shake the sensation of being watched. "Like the whole world knows what we've done."

A chill wind whispered through the alleyways, carrying with it the scent of ozone and decay. In the distance, thunder rumbled – a storm gathering, mirroring the tempest of our souls.

"We've opened Pandora's box," I said, the words tasting like ashes in my mouth. "And now we're the only ones who can close it."

Jessica's grip tightened. "Whatever it takes," she vowed.

As we walked into the gathering gloom, I couldn't help but wonder: What terrible price would we have to pay to set things right? And would we be strong enough to pay for it?

Chapter 3

Meeting the Mentor

I leaned closer to the ancient tome, its musty pages crackling beneath my trembling fingers. Michael's breath tickled my ear as he whispered, "What do you make of these symbols, Jess?"

I traced the arcane glyphs with a fingertip. "They almost look like... constellations. But warped, twisted somehow." A chill slithered down my spine. What dark secrets lay hidden in this text?

"Maybe they're some kind of star map," Michael mused. "To guide travellers between realms?"

I nodded absently, lost in the swirling patterns. They seemed to write on the page, hinting at cosmic horrors beyond mortal comprehension. Part of me longed to slam the book shut, to flee from the forbidden knowledge contained within. But a deeper, darker part of me hungered to know more.

"There's something... alive about them," I murmured. "Can't you feel it?"

Michael shifted uneasily beside me. "I don't like this, Jess. Maybe we should—"

His words died as an icy wind gusted through our stuffy apartment. Goosebumps prickled my flesh. The candles guttered, plunging us into shadow.

"Did you leave a window open?" I asked, my voice quivering.

Michael shook his head, eyes darting about the room. "No, I... what was that?"

The temperature plummeted. Our ragged breaths misted in the suddenly frigid air. The shadows in the corners seemed to deepen, to writhe with unholy life.

My heart pounded. We had awakened something with our meddling; I was sure of it. Some slumbering entity from beyond the veil of reality. And now it had come for us, drawn by our foolish curiosity.

I clutched Michael's arm. "We need to get out of here. Now."

But even as the words left my lips, I knew it was too late. We were no longer alone.

A shimmer rippled through the air as if reality itself were bending. My eyes widened in disbelief as a figure materialized before us, her presence both unsettling and mesmerizing.

"Michael," I whispered, my voice barely audible. "Do you see...?"

But I couldn't tear my gaze away to check his reaction. The woman – if she could be called that – stood tall and ethereal, her silver hair cascading like moonlight. And her eyes... oh, her eyes. Deep violet pools that seemed to hold the very secrets of the cosmos.

"Thalia Moonshadow," the name slipped unbidden from my lips, though I couldn't fathom how I knew it.

Michael stumbled backward, his face a mask of shock. "This can't be real," he muttered. "We must be hallucinating."

But I felt myself drawn forward, an inexplicable pull urging me closer to this otherworldly being. My mind reeled, torn between terror and an overwhelming sense of... recognition. It was as if I'd been waiting my entire life for this moment, without ever knowing it.

"Who are you?" I asked, my voice trembling. "What do you want from us?"

Thalia's gaze bore into mine, and I felt laid bare before her, all my secrets and fears exposed. A chill ran down my spine, but I couldn't look away. What dark truths did those violet eyes see within me?

Thalia's lips parted, and a voice like silk on stone filled the room. "Jessica," she breathed, my name a melody on her tongue. "Michael. The stars have whispered of your coming."

Her words echoed, not just in the confines of our cramped apartment but within the very core of my being. I shivered, feeling the weight of destiny settling upon my shoulders like a shroud.

"What... what do you mean?" I stammered, fighting the urge to fall to my knees before her.

Thalia's gaze softened, but the intensity remained. "In the tapestry of fate, your threads shine bright," she intoned, her speech falling into a hypnotic rhythm. "But beware, for brilliance casts the darkest shadows."

Michael found his voice, skepticism battling with awe. "That doesn't answer anything. Who are you? How did you get here?"

I wanted to hush him, to bask in the enigma of Thalia's presence, but a part of me clung to his practicality. It was the only thing keeping me tethered to reality.

Thalia's smile was a crescent moon, beautiful and remote. "I am the keeper of whispers, the bridge between realms," she said. "And you, dear ones, stand at the precipice of a cosmic awakening."

Her words washed over me, each one a puzzle piece I couldn't quite fit together. What cosmic awakening? What did she want from us? And why did I feel like I'd been waiting for this moment my entire life?

"Please," I whispered, "speak plainly. We don't understand."

But even as I begged for clarity, a part of me reveled in the mystery. What dark secrets lay hidden in Thalia's cryptic words? And more terrifying still – what truths about myself would this journey reveal?

Thalia's violet eyes flickered to the ancient text lying open on our cluttered desk. A shiver ran down my spine as she spoke, her voice carrying the weight of eons.

"That tome you possess," she said, "it's no mere relic. It's a key —a bridge between worlds. Within its pages lies the power to summon the dragons back to Earth."

My breath caught in my throat. Dragons? Surely, she couldn't mean...

"The world teeters on the brink of catastrophe," Thalia continued, urgency seeping into her melodic tones. "Only the dragons' return can restore balance."

I glanced at Michael, his face a mirror of my own bewilderment. Yet beneath the shock, I saw a spark of something else— determination, maybe even excitement.

"Why us?" I asked, my voice barely above a whisper. "We're nobody special."

Thalia's gaze pierced through me as if reading the darkest corners of my soul. "Destiny rarely calls upon the qualified, Jessica. It favors the willing."

Those words resonated within me, stirring something long dormant. I turned to Michael, our eyes locking in silent communication. At that moment, I saw my own mix of fear and resolve reflected in his gaze.

We didn't need to speak. The weight of responsibility settled upon our shoulders like a tangible thing, heavy yet oddly exhilarating. What terrors would we face? What sacrifices would be demanded of us?

As the gravity of our task sank in, I couldn't shake the feeling that we'd just stepped off the edge of a cliff. There was no going back now—only the long fall into whatever fate awaited us.

Thalia glided closer, her ethereal form seeming to shimmer at the edges. The air around her crackled with an energy I couldn't quite comprehend, both alluring and terrifying in its intensity. She extended a slender hand toward the ancient text, her fingertips barely grazing its weathered surface.

"The secrets within these pages are not for the faint of heart," she murmured her voice a hypnotic cadence that sent shivers down my spine. "To decipher them is to dance with shadows long forgotten."

I swallowed hard, my mouth suddenly dry. "How... how do we begin?"

Thalia's violet eyes locked onto mine, and for a moment, I felt as if I were drowning in pools of cosmic mystery. "Listen to the whispers between the words," she advised. "Feel the pulse of magic that thrums beneath each symbol."

Michael leaned forward; his brow furrowed in concentration. "It's like they're... moving," he muttered, squinting at the page.

I saw it, too—or thought I did. The intricate patterns seemed to writhe and twist, forming fleeting images that vanished as quickly as they appeared: dragons soaring through star-filled skies, great battles waged across distant worlds, and civilizations rising and falling in the blink of an eye.

My mind reeled, struggling to process the barrage of information. What if we failed? What if we unleashed something we couldn't control? The weight of countless lives pressed down upon me, threatening to crush my resolve.

"The path ahead is treacherous," Thalia intoned, her words cutting through my spiraling thoughts. "But remember, even in the darkest night, starlight finds a way to shine."

I turned away, my heart pounding in my chest like a caged bird desperate for escape. The ancient text blurred before my eyes, its secrets mocking me with their impenetrable silence. How could I, Jessica, a mere mortal with trembling hands and a racing mind, possibly hope to unravel the mysteries of dragons and cosmic realms?

"I can't do this," I whispered, the words slipping out unbidden. My lower lip found its way between my teeth, a familiar comfort in this sea of uncertainty. "What if I make a mistake? What if I doom us all?"

The weight of responsibility settled upon my shoulders, a crushing burden that threatened to drive me to my knees. I closed my eyes, trying to shut out the world, but visions of calamity danced behind my eyelids – cities reduced to ash, skies torn asunder, the very fabric of reality unraveling at my fumbling touch.

"Jessica," Michael's voice cut through the maelstrom of my thoughts, steady as a rock in a storm-tossed sea. I felt his warm hand envelop mine, his calloused fingers intertwining with my own. "Look at me."

I opened my eyes, meeting his gaze. In those depths of warm brown, I saw not judgment or disappointment but unwavering faith. "We're in this together," he murmured, his thumb tracing soothing circles on the back of my hand. "Every step of the way."

The simple gesture spoke volumes, anchoring me in the present moment. I drew a shaky breath, feeling some of the tension ease from my shoulders. "But what if—"

"No what-ifs," Michael interrupted gently. "We'll face whatever comes, side by side. That's how we've always done it, remember?"

A ghost of a smile tugged at my lips as memories of past trials flooded my mind. We had weathered storms before, hadn't we? Perhaps not on this scale, but still...

"Together," I echoed, my voice barely above a whisper. The word hung in the air between us, a fragile promise in the face of cosmic forces beyond our comprehension.

I felt Thalia's gaze upon us, her violet eyes shimmering with an otherworldly light. A chill crawled up my spine as she nodded, her enigmatic smile both alluring and unsettling.

"Your bond," she murmured, her voice like moonlight on water, "it will be your greatest strength in the trials to come."

I couldn't shake the feeling that her words held layers of meaning, secrets coiled within secrets. "What aren't you telling us?" I asked, my voice trembling despite my efforts to steady it.

Thalia's smile deepened, revealing nothing. "The path ahead is shrouded in shadow, dear one. But know this – you do not walk it alone."

Her presence, once intimidating, now felt oddly comforting.

A beacon of hope in the encroaching darkness. Yet even as that thought formed, I felt her slipping away.

"Wait!" I cried, reaching out. But it was too late.

Thalia's form shimmered, dissolving like mist in the morning sun. In the blink of an eye, she was gone, leaving Michael and me alone in our dimly lit apartment.

The silence that followed was deafening. I turned to Michael, seeing my own mix of awe and trepidation mirrored in his eyes. "Did that really just happen?" I whispered.

He nodded slowly. "I think... I think our lives just changed forever."

The weight of our mission pressed down upon me, threatening to crush my resolve. But beneath the fear, a tiny spark of excitement flickered to life. We weren't alone. Whatever lay ahead, we had an ally in the enigmatic Thalia Moonshadow.

I squeezed Michael's hand, drawing strength from his unwavering presence. "Well," I said, my voice steadier than I felt, "I suppose we'd better get to work on deciphering that text."

I turned back to the ancient tome, its weathered pages now seeming to pulse with an otherworldly energy. My fingers trembled as I traced the cryptic symbols, their meaning just beyond my grasp.

"Do you think we can really do this?" I murmured more to myself than to Michael.

He leaned in close, his breath warm on my neck. "We have to try, Jess. For the sake of everything."

I nodded, swallowing hard. The magnitude of our task threatened to overwhelm me, but I pushed the feeling down. "Right. Let's start with the first page."

As we pored over the text, the shadows in the room seemed to deepen, creeping closer. I shivered, unable to shake the feeling that we were being watched.

"Michael," I whispered, "do you feel that?"

He paused, frowning. "Like... like we're not alone?"

I nodded, my heart racing. "It's probably nothing. Just nerves, right?"

But even as I spoke, a chill ran down my spine. The air grew thick and heavy with unspoken secrets. What horrors had we unwittingly unleashed?

"Keep reading," I urged, my voice hoarse. "We can't stop now."

The words on the page blurred, shifting like smoke. Were they changing, or was my mind playing tricks? I blinked hard, trying to focus.

"Jess," Michael's voice was tight with tension, "I think I found something."

I leaned in, my breath catching as I saw what he had uncovered: a map hidden within the text itself. A path to... what?

"The Ethereal Realm," I breathed, the words tasting of stardust and ancient magic.

Our eyes met a silent understanding passing between us. Whatever lay ahead, whatever darkness we must face, we would face it together.

The chapter of our old lives was closing. A new one, fraught with peril and promise, was just beginning.

CHAPTER 4

TRAINING

I hesitated at the threshold, my breath catching in my throat. The sanctuary before us pulsed with an otherworldly energy that made my skin prickle. Michael's hand found mine, his fingers trembling slightly against my palm. We exchanged a glance, his eyes mirroring the mix of wonder and fear I felt churning in my gut.

"We've come this far," I whispered, willing my voice not to crack. "No turning back now."

We stepped into the dimly lit chamber, shadows dancing at the edges of my vision. The air grew thick, and heavy with the scent of ancient magic and whispered secrets. My heart thundered in my chest as my gaze fell upon her - Thalia Moonshadow.

She stood motionless in the center of the room, tall and ethereal. Her silver hair cascaded like liquid moonlight over her shoulders, and her violet eyes seemed to pierce through to my very soul. A shiver ran down my spine. Those eyes had seen eternity.

Thalia's lips curved into the faintest smile as she inclined her head in greeting. "Welcome, seekers of truth," she intoned, her voice as soft as a night breeze yet resonating with quiet power. "You stand now at the precipice of revelation."

I swallowed hard, fighting the urge to flee. What terrible truths awaited us here? What sins of the past would be laid bare?

"We seek your guidance, Enigmatic Seer," Michael said, his voice steadier than I had expected.

Thalia's gaze shifted to him, and I felt him stiffen beside me. "Knowledge comes at a price, young one," she murmured. "Are you prepared to pay it?"

The air grew colder, and tendrils of dread curled around my heart. What price would be demanded of us? I thought of the shadows that had haunted my dreams, the whispers of cosmic horror that echoed in the darkest corners of my mind. Were we truly ready to face what lay ahead?

Thalia's eyes found mine once more, and I saw eternity reflected in their depths. "The path you walk is treacherous," she said, her words carrying the weight of prophecy. "The fate of worlds hangs in the balance. Are you prepared to bear that burden?"

I wanted to say no, to turn and run from this place of ancient power and forgotten truths. But something deeper, some primal instinct, kept me rooted to the spot. "We are," I heard myself say, my voice barely above a whisper.

A sad smile touched Thalia's lips. "Then let us begin," she said softly. "For the hour grows late, and the darkness gathers."

As she spoke, the shadows in the room seemed to deepen, and I felt the weight of destiny settling upon my shoulders. Whatever lay ahead, I knew with grim certainty that we would never be the same again.

Thalia's ethereal form glided toward us, her silver hair shimmering like starlight. "Close your eyes," she commanded her voice a haunting melody that seemed to resonate within my very bones. "Let the veil of the mundane world fall away."

I hesitated, fear gnawing at my insides. What horrors might I see with my inner eye? But Michael's steady presence beside me gave me courage, and I allowed my eyelids to flutter shut.

"Breathe deeply," Thalia intoned. "Feel the pulse of the cosmos thrumming through your veins."

As I inhaled, the air felt thick and heavy with an ancient power that made my skin prickle. With each breath, I sensed a change within me, as if long-dormant senses were awakening.

"Listen," Thalia whispered, her words seeming to come from everywhere and nowhere at once. "Hear the whispers of forgotten magic."

At first, there was only silence. But then, faintly, I began to perceive something: ghostly murmurs, like the echoes of long-dead voices brushing against my consciousness. I shuddered, recognizing words in languages that had never graced mortal tongues.

"What is this?" I gasped, my eyes flying open in panic. "These voices—they speak of terrible things."

Thalia's gaze met mine, unfathomable depths of knowledge swirling in her violet eyes. "The price of power," she said softly, "is to bear witness to truths that others cannot face."

I swallowed hard, fighting back the urge to flee. "And if those truths drive us mad?"

A sad smile touched Thalia's lips. "Then perhaps madness is the key to unlocking the mysteries of the universe."

Thalia's enigmatic smile lingered as she settled into a cross-legged position before us. The air shimmered around her as if reality itself bent to her will.

"To understand your task," she began, her voice a melodic whisper, "you must first know the dragons."

I leaned forward, drawn in despite myself. The whispers still echoed in my mind, a cacophony of ancient terrors.

"In the beginning," Thalia intoned, "there was only void and starlight. From this primordial chaos, the dragons emerged."

As she spoke, I could almost see it—vast, serpentine forms coalescing from stardust, their scales glittering with the light of newborn galaxies.

"They were guardians," Thalia continued, "tasked with maintaining the balance between order and entropy."

My breath caught. Guardians. Just like us. The weight of that legacy pressed down on me, threatening to crush my spirit.

"But... how can we possibly live up to that?" I blurted out, my voice cracking. "We're just... us."

Thalia's gaze pierced me, seeing through my feeble bravado. "Doubt is the shadow cast by greatness," she murmured. "It is the price of potential."

I clenched my fists, nails biting into my palms. The pain grounded me, a reminder of my mortal flesh, even as my mind reeled with cosmic truths.

"I'm not ready," I whispered, more to myself than to anyone else.

Michael's hand found mine, a warm anchor in the tempest of my thoughts. "None of us are," he said softly. "But we're all we've got."

I closed my eyes, breathing deeply. The whispers surged, a tide of ancient knowledge threatening to drown me. But beneath it all, I felt something else. A spark. A flame.

My eyes snapped open, meeting Thalia's knowing gaze. "Tell us more," I said, my voice steadier than I felt. "We need to know everything."

The air grew thick, charged with an unseen energy that made my skin prickle. Thalia rose, her silver hair catching the ethereal light as she moved to the center of the chamber.

"Watch closely," she intoned, her voice a haunting melody. "The veil between worlds is thin here. We must tread carefully."

I leaned forward, my heart racing. Thalia's hands began to weave intricate patterns in the air, leaving faint trails of silvery light. The whispers in my mind grew louder and more insistent.

"What do you see?" Michael murmured beside me, his eyes wide.

"I... I'm not sure," I breathed, transfixed by Thalia's fluid movements. Each gesture seemed to ripple through the very fabric of reality.

Suddenly, the air before Thalia shimmered like heat rising from sun-baked stone. A small orb of light coalesced between her palms, pulsing with an otherworldly rhythm.

"This is but a fraction of the power that flows through the veins of our world," Thalia said, her voice echoing strangely. "Now, Michael. You will attempt the ritual."

Michael stood, his face a mask of determination that couldn't quite hide the fear in his eyes. As he stepped forward, I felt a sharp pang of... was it jealousy? Or relief that I wasn't first?

"Remember," Thalia cautioned, "intention is key. The magic responds to your will, but it is not yours to command."

Michael nodded, his hands shaking as he raised them. He began to mimic Thalia's movements, his gestures clumsy and hesitant at first. The air around him began to crackle, faint sparks dancing at his fingertips.

I watched, mesmerized and terrified. What if he couldn't do it? What if I couldn't? The weight of our task pressed down on me once more, a smothering blanket of doubt.

But as Michael continued, his movements grew more assured. The sparks intensified, coalescing into flickering tendrils of light. His face was a study in concentration, beads of sweat forming on his brow.

"Good," Thalia murmured, her eyes never leaving Michael's hands. "Now, focus your intent. What do you wish to manifest?"

Michael's brow furrowed. The tendrils of light writhed and twisted as if fighting against an invisible force. I held my breath, my own hands clenched so tightly that I could feel my nails cutting into my palms.

The chamber fell silent, save for the soft hum of magic and the ragged sound of Michael's breathing. Time seemed to stretch, each second an eternity of anticipation and dread.

And then, in a sudden burst of radiance, a small orb of light blossomed in Michael's palm. It pulsed gently, casting a warm glow across his face. His eyes widened, disbelief giving way to a tentative smile.

"I... I did it," he whispered, his voice thick with emotion.

I felt a surge of pride for him, tinged with a gnawing envy. Would I be able to match his success?

"Well done," Thalia said, her tone betraying nothing. "Jessica, you're next."

My heart plummeted. I stepped forward, my legs leaden. The weight of expectation pressed down on me, threatening to crush what little confidence I had left.

I raised my hands, mimicking the gestures Thalia had shown us. Nothing happened. No sparks, no tingling, nothing but the oppressive silence of the chamber.

"Concentrate," Thalia urged. "Find the magic within you."

I closed my eyes, searching for something, anything: a flicker of warmth, a spark of power. But there was only darkness, cold and unyielding.

"I can't," I choked out. "It's not working."

"Try again," Thalia commanded. Was that disappointment in her voice? Or something worse?

I gritted my teeth, forcing my hands through the motions once more. This time, I felt it - a faint stirring, like the first breath of wind before a storm.

"That's it," Michael encouraged. "You've got this, Jess."

I latched onto that tiny spark, willing it to grow. Slowly, painfully, a dim light began to form in my palm. It flickered weakly, threatening to extinguish at any moment.

But I held on, pouring every ounce of determination into that fragile light. And with each passing second, it grew brighter.

The light in my palm pulsed, growing brighter with each heartbeat. Thalia's violet eyes gleamed in the ethereal glow, her expression inscrutable.

"Good," she murmured, her voice a soft caress. "Now, reach deeper. There are hidden depths within you, Jessica. Untapped reservoirs of power waiting to be unleashed."

I closed my eyes, focusing inward. The darkness behind my eyelids swirled, punctuated by flashes of starlight. Was this the cosmic energy Thalia spoke of?

"Let go of your doubts," Thalia urged. "They are chains binding your true potential."

My mind raced, filled with questions and fears. What if I wasn't strong enough? What if I failed?

"Silence those thoughts," Thalia commanded as if reading my mind. "They are but echoes of past failures. You stand on the precipice of greatness. Will you take the leap?"

I took a deep breath, pushing away the whispers of self-doubt. The light in my hand flared, bright enough to cast shadows on the chamber walls.

"Remarkable," Michael whispered, awe evident in his voice.

Later, as we rested, Michael and I huddled in a corner of the sanctuary, our voices hushed.

"I never imagined I could do something like that," he confessed, his eyes wide with wonder and a hint of fear.

I nodded, understanding all too well. "It's terrifying, isn't it? To hold that much power in your hands?"

"And exhilarating," Michael added with a nervous laugh. "Do you think we're ready for what's coming?"

I glanced at Thalia, who stood motionless across the room, her gaze fixed on some distant point beyond our comprehension.

"I don't know," I admitted. "But I'm glad we're in this together."

As the ethereal light faded from our hands, Thalia approached, her footsteps silent on the ancient stone floor. The air grew thick with anticipation, a palpable weight settling upon my shoulders.

"You've taken your first steps into a realm beyond mortal comprehension," Thalia intoned, her violet eyes piercing through the dimness. "But remember, with great power comes a burden that will test the very essence of your being."

I shuddered, her words seeping into my bones like a cold mist.

"What if we're not strong enough?" I whispered, the question escaping my lips before I could stop it.

Thalia's gaze softened, a flicker of something—was it pity?—crossing her ageless features. "Strength is not measured in magical prowess alone, Jessica. It is the resolve in your heart that will determine your fate."

Michael shifted beside me, his presence a comforting warmth in the chill of the sanctuary. "And what of our mission?" he asked, his voice steady despite the tremor I felt in his hand.

Thalia's lips curved into a smile that didn't quite reach her eyes. "Your path is written in the stars, intertwined with the very fabric of existence. Remember this: in the darkest of nights, it is not the absence of light that should frighten you, but the shadows that lurk within your own soul."

Her words hung in the air, a haunting melody that echoed in the chambers of my mind. As we turned to leave, I caught a glimpse of our reflections in a polished obsidian wall—two figures, once ordinary, now touched by the arcane. Our steps were measured, more assured than when we had entered, yet I couldn't shake the feeling that we were walking a knife's edge between destiny and doom.

The weight of our newfound knowledge pressed upon us, a constant reminder of the monumental task that lay ahead. As we crossed the threshold of Thalia's sanctuary, I cast one last glance over my shoulder. For a moment, I swore I saw a flicker of sorrow in Thalia's eyes, gone as quickly as it appeared, leaving me to wonder what terrible secrets she still held close to her heart.

The path ahead stretched before us, a tapestry of shadows and starlight. I couldn't shake the feeling that each step drew us deeper into a labyrinth of cosmic mysteries, with Thalia as our enigmatic Ariadne.

"Michael," I whispered, my voice barely audible above the whisper of wind through ethereal trees, "do you think we're ready for what comes next?"

He turned to me, his eyes reflecting pinpricks of celestial light.

"Ready? I'm not sure anyone could be truly ready for this, Jess. But we don't have a choice, do we?"

I nodded, a chill creeping up my spine that had nothing to do with the cool night air. "I keep hearing Thalia's words in my head about the shadows within our souls. What if... what if we're not strong enough to face them?"

Michael's hand found mine warm and reassuring. "Then we face them together. Whatever comes."

As we walked, the very air seemed to pulse with potential, with secrets yet to be unveiled. I couldn't shake the feeling that we were being watched, not just by Thalia, but by something more ancient, more terrible. The weight of unspoken prophecies hung heavy in the air, a promise of trials that would test not just our newfound abilities but the very essence of who we were.

What revelations awaited us in the cosmic dance of dragons? What price would we pay for the power to shape destiny? These questions echoed in the hollow of my chest, a drumbeat of anticipation and dread.

I cast one last look at the sanctuary, now shrouded in mist. Thalia's final words whispered through my mind: "The path of light oft casts the darkest shadows." A shiver ran through me, and I turned away, steeling myself for the challenges that lay ahead in the starry dominion of dragons and fate.

CHAPTER 5

FIRST CHALLENGE

The ancient stone archway loomed before us, its jagged edges like teeth ready to devour. I exchanged a glance with Michael, his eyes mirroring the dread that gnawed at my insides. We had come too far to turn back now.

"Ready?" I whispered, my voice barely audible over the pounding of my heart.

Michael nodded, his jaw set with grim determination. "As we'll ever be."

We stepped through the threshold, and immediately, the air thickened, pressing down on us with the weight of forgotten centuries. An oppressive energy seeped into my bones, chilling me to my core. The sanctuary stretched out before us, vast and empty, yet I couldn't shake the feeling of being watched.

"Do you feel that?" I murmured, fighting to keep my voice steady.

"Like a thousand eyes boring into my soul," Michael replied, his words tinged with unease.

I scanned the shadows, searching for any sign of movement, but found only stillness. The silence was deafening, broken only by our shallow breathing and the echo of our footsteps on cold stone.

My mind raced with doubts and fears. What horrors had we awakened? What price would we pay for our hubris? The weight of our past decisions bore down on me, threatening to crush my resolve.

"Jessica," Michael's voice cut through my spiraling thoughts. "We can't falter now. Whatever lies ahead, we face it together."

I nodded, drawing strength from his words, even as a part of me whispered that we were fools to think we could emerge from this unscathed. The sanctuary's oppressive atmosphere seemed to feed on our fears, growing stronger with each passing moment.

As we ventured deeper into the heart of our self-made nightmare, I couldn't help but wonder: had we damned ourselves in our quest for knowledge? Only time would tell, and in this forsaken place, time seemed to hold its breath, waiting to reveal our fate.

The corridor narrowed, forcing us to press closer together. Our footsteps echoed ominously, and each sound a betrayal of our presence in this hallowed, forsaken place. Ahead, a yawning darkness loomed - the entrance to the labyrinth, a gaping maw ready to swallow us whole.

"There it is," I whispered, my voice barely audible even to my own ears. "Our path to revelation... or damnation."

Michael's hand found mine, his grip firm yet trembling. "We've come too far to turn back now."

As we approached the threshold, tendrils of shadow seemed to reach out, caressing our skin with icy fingers. I clutched the ancient text to my chest, its weight both comforting and terrifying. Would its cryptic passages guide us through the maze or lead us further astray?

"Ready?" Michael asked, his eyes reflecting the same mix of determination and fear I felt coursing through my veins.

I nodded, not trusting my voice. Together, we stepped into the abyss.

The moment we crossed the threshold, the world shifted.

Walls twisted and contorted, defying all logic. The path behind us vanished, leaving only an ever-changing labyrinth ahead.

"God," I breathed, fighting the rising panic in my chest. "It's alive."

Michael's grip on my hand tightened. "Stay close. We can't afford to be separated."

I fumbled with the ancient text, my fingers trembling as I tried to decipher its faded script. "There must be something here, some clue to guide us."

As we navigated the shifting corridors, each turn brought new horrors to mind. What unspeakable trials awaited us? And more terrifying still - were we truly prepared to face the truths we sought?

The labyrinth seemed to pulse around us, a living entity feeding on our fears and doubts. With each step, I felt the weight of our past choices bearing down, threatening to crush what little hope remained.

A chill wind whispered through the corridor, carrying with it the faint scent of decay. I shivered, my skin prickling with an unnatural cold.

"Jessica," Michael's voice was tight, "do you see them?"

I looked up from the ancient text, my breath catching in my throat. Shadows danced on the walls, coalescing into ethereal forms that flickered and twisted in impossible ways. They swarmed toward us, their incorporeal bodies radiating malevolence.

"Spectral entities," I hissed, my mind racing through half-remembered lessons. "We need to combine our magic, Michael. Remember what I taught you about energy manipulation?"

He nodded, his face pale but determined. "I think so. Like this?" He extended his hand, a faint blue light emanating from his fingertips.

"Close," I said, adjusting his stance. "Channel it through your core, not just your extremities."

As the ethereal creatures drew nearer, I felt the familiar surge of power coursing through me. "Now, Michael!"

We released our magic in unison, a blinding flash of light erupting between us. The spectral swarm recoiled, their otherworldly shrieks echoing off the labyrinth walls.

"It's working," Michael gasped, his voice strained with effort. "But there are so many of them."

I gritted my teeth, pushing more energy into our combined spell. "Focus, Michael. We can't falter now."

The battle raged on, each wave of spirits more relentless than the last. Just when I thought we might be overwhelmed, the swarm dissipated, leaving us alone in the eerie silence of the maze.

Michael slumped against the wall, sweat beading on his brow. "That was... intense."

I nodded, my own limbs trembling from exertion. "You did well. Better than I expected, honestly."

He managed a weak smile. "Thanks, I think."

As we caught our breath, the labyrinth shifted once more. The path ahead split into three identical corridors, each emanating a soft, pulsing light.

"Another test," I muttered, scanning the ancient text for guidance. "We need to choose wisely."

Michael peered down each passage. "They all look the same to me. How do we know which is safe?"

I closed my eyes, reaching out with my senses. "We don't. That's the point. This trap isn't about finding the right path - it's about trusting our instincts."

"Well," Michael said, his voice wavering, "your instincts are probably better than mine. What do you think?"

I hesitated, the weight of the decision pressing down on me. "I... I'm not sure. What if I choose wrong?"

Michael placed a hand on my shoulder. "Then we face it together. That's why we're here, right?"

His words stirred something within me - a flicker of hope

amidst the encroaching darkness. I took a deep breath, steeling myself for whatever lay ahead.

"The middle path," I said, my voice steadier than I felt. "It feels... right, somehow."

As we stepped forward, I couldn't shake the feeling that our true test was only just beginning.

The corridor narrowed as we pressed on, the walls seeming to close in around us. Each step echoed ominously, a grim reminder of our isolation in this forsaken place. The air grew thick and oppressive as if the very essence of the labyrinth sought to crush our resolve.

"Jessica," Michael whispered, his voice strained, "do you really think we can do this?"

I turned to him, catching the flicker of doubt in his eyes. It mirrored my own fears, threatening to overwhelm me. "I... I don't know," I admitted, the words tasting bitter on my tongue. "But we have to try, don't we?"

He nodded, but I could see the weight of our mission bearing down on him. I reached for his hand, finding it clammy and trembling.

"What if we're not strong enough?" I voiced the fear that had been gnawing at me. "What if we fail, and everyone—"

"Don't," Michael interrupted, his grip tightening. "We can't think like that. We—"

His words cut off as we stumbled into a vast chamber. The walls shimmered, rippling like water, and suddenly, we were surrounded by reflections of ourselves. But these weren't mere mirrors—they showed us our darkest fears and our deepest regrets.

I saw myself alone and powerless, watching helplessly as our world crumbled. Michael's reflection showed him consumed by the very magic we sought to control, his humanity slipping away.

"It's not real," I gasped, fighting against the panic rising in my chest. "Michael, it's just illusions. We have to—"

But Michael was transfixed, his eyes wide with horror as he

stared at his corrupted reflection. I grabbed his shoulders, forcing him to look at me.

"Remember why we're here," I pleaded, my voice breaking. "Remember what we're fighting for."

For a moment, I thought I'd lost him to the nightmares. Then his eyes cleared, focusing on mine. "Together," he whispered, a ghost of a smile on his lips.

We clung to each other, shutting out the terrifying visions that surrounded us. In that moment of connection, I felt a surge of strength. The illusions began to fade, dissipating like mist in the morning sun.

As the chamber returned to normal, I realized that our greatest power wasn't in the magic we wielded but in the bond we shared. Whatever horrors lay ahead, we would face them united.

I stumbled forward, my legs still weak from the ordeal we'd just endured. The narrow corridor suddenly opened into a vast, cavernous hall. My breath caught in my throat.

"Jessica," Michael whispered, his voice tinged with awe and fear. "Look."

Before us stood a creature unlike anything I'd ever seen. It towered over us, its form shifting and undulating like smoke-given life. Eyes—countless eyes—blinked open and closed across its ethereal body. The weight of its gaze pressed down upon us, threatening to crush our very souls.

"We've come this far," I murmured, more to steady myself than to reassure Michael. "We can't turn back now."

The guardian's voice reverberated through the chamber, each word a physical force that made my bones ache. "You seek passage," it intoned. "But are you worthy?"

I swallowed hard, fighting the urge to flee. "We are," I declared, hoping my voice didn't betray my terror.

"Then prove it," the creature demanded. "Show me the truth of your hearts."

Suddenly, I felt naked, exposed. Not physically, but as if every dark thought, every selfish desire, and every moment of weakness was laid bare before this ancient being.

"I-I'm afraid," I admitted, the words tumbling out unbidden. "Afraid I'm not strong enough. That I'll fail everyone who's counting on us."

Michael's hand found mine, squeezing gently. "And I'm afraid of losing myself," he confessed. "Of becoming something I won't recognize."

The guardian's eyes narrowed, piercing through us. "Fear," it mused. "The seed of both cowardice and courage. Which will you nurture?"

I closed my eyes, searching for an answer within myself. When I opened them again, I met the guardian's gaze with newfound resolve.

"We choose courage," I said, my voice steadier than I felt. "Because the world needs us to be more than our fears."

The guardian's form shimmered, its edges blurring like smoke in the wind. "Courage... and honesty," it murmured, its voice now softer, almost contemplative. "Rare treasures in these dark times."

I felt Michael's grip tighten on my hand. His presence anchored me, a lifeline in this sea of uncertainty. "We've come too far to turn back now," he said, echoing my earlier words. "Whatever the cost, we'll see this through."

A wave of warmth washed over me, born of Michael's unwavering faith. It mingled with my own determination, growing into something greater than either of us alone.

"Very well," the guardian intoned. "You may pass."

The air itself seemed to sigh, the oppressive weight that had dogged our steps since entering the labyrinth lifting like a veil. As we stepped past the guardian, I caught a glimpse of something in its eyes - approval, perhaps? Or was it hope?

We emerged into a corridor bathed in soft, starry light. The walls no longer felt like prison bars but rather protective sentinels guiding our way.

"We did it," I breathed, scarcely daring to believe. "Michael, we actually did it."

He smiled a rare sight that never failed to make my heart skip. "We did," he agreed. "Together."

As we walked, each step felt lighter than the last. The trials we'd faced, the fears we'd confronted - they'd forged something between us, stronger than steel and more precious than gold.

"Do you think..." I hesitated, old doubts threatening to resurface. "Do you think we're ready for what comes next?"

Michael's answer was simple, but it rang with conviction. "I think we're as ready as we'll ever be."

And in that moment, surrounded by the ethereal glow of the Cosmic Sanctuary, I allowed myself to believe him.

I closed my eyes, inhaling the crisp scent of stardust that permeated the air. The cosmic melodies that had once seemed so alien now whispered to me like old friends, their haunting refrains echoing the trials we'd endured.

"We've changed," I murmured, more to myself than to Michael.

He caught my gaze, his blue eyes piercing in the gentle luminescence. "For better or worse?"

A wry smile twisted my lips. "Both, I think. The labyrinth... it peeled back layers I didn't know I had."

Michael nodded, his expression grave. "I saw things in there, Jess. Things I'm not proud of."

"We all have our demons," I replied, reaching for his hand. The warmth of his skin against mine was an anchor, grounding me in the vastness of the Ethereal Realm.

As we approached the sanctuary's exit, a chill crept up my spine. The weight of our mission, momentarily forgotten in the aftermath of our triumph, settled back onto our shoulders like a funeral shroud.

"What if we fail?" The words escaped before I could stop them; my voice was barely a whisper.

Michael's grip on my hand tightened. "Then we fail together," he said, his tone brooking no argument. "But we won't."

I wanted to believe him. Oh, how I wanted to believe! But the path ahead loomed dark and treacherous, a maze far more complex than the one we'd just escaped.

"Ready?" Michael asked as we stood before the shimmering portal that would return us to our world.

I nodded, steeling myself. "Ready."

Together, we stepped through, leaving the starry dominion behind. But its magic clung to us still, a silent promise of the power that lay dormant within our souls.

The familiar scent of pine and damp earth assaulted my senses as we materialized in the shadowy forest. Twilight had descended, casting long, menacing shadows that seemed to reach for us with grasping fingers. I shivered; the sanctuary's warmth was already a fading memory.

"We should make camp," Michael murmured, his eyes darting warily between the trees. "It's not safe to travel at night."

I nodded, my throat too tight for words. The weight of the ancient text in my pack felt heavier than ever, its secrets now intertwined with our own.

As Michael busied himself gathering firewood, I sank to the forest floor, my mind reeling. The labyrinth's visions still haunted me, whispers of failure and betrayal echoing in the rustling leaves.

"Jess?" Michael's voice cut through my spiraling thoughts. "You're trembling."

I forced a weak smile. "Just cold," I lied, knowing he could see right through me.

He knelt beside me, his warmth a stark contrast to the chill air. "We're going to summon those dragons," he said firmly. "We're going to save our world."

"And if we can't?" The words tasted like ash on my tongue.

Michael's eyes hardened, a determination I'd never seen before blazing in their depths. "Then we'll die trying."

As the flames of our small fire licked at the encroaching darkness, I clung to that resolve, willing it to burn away my doubts. But in the shadows beyond our circle of light, I could have sworn I saw figures moving, watching... waiting.

CHAPTER 6

GATHERING ALLIES

The flickering torchlight cast long shadows as we crept into the abandoned cathedral. My heart pounded, each beat a reminder of our desperate mission. Jessica and Michael flanked me, their faces grim masks in the gloom.

"Quite the cheery spot for a clandestine meeting," I murmured, my voice echoing in the cavernous space. "One might almost forget the demons at our heels."

A chuckle rang out, startling us. "Well, if it isn't the doomsday brigade, right on schedule."

From behind a crumbling pillar stepped a man with tousled brown hair and eyes that danced with mischief: Kael Stoneforge, the infamous Arcane Trickster. His grin was sharp enough to cut.

"Fashionably late as always, Kael," I said, fighting a smirk. His levity was a balm to my frayed nerves, though I'd never admit it.

He swept into an exaggerated bow. "My dear Thalia, one must maintain an air of mystery. It keeps things interesting, wouldn't you agree?"

I rolled my eyes but couldn't quite suppress the smile tugging at my lips. Kael's charm was as potent as his magic - and just as dangerous.

Jessica stepped forward, her voice tight. "If you're quite finished with the theatrics, we have urgent matters to discuss."

"Ah yes, the impending doom and all that," Kael said airily, though his eyes had lost some of their sparkle. "Well then, shall we get down to business? I do so love a good apocalypse-averting strategy session."

As the others began to speak, I found my gaze drawn to the shadows lurking in the corners of the cathedral. What secrets did they hide? What whispers of prophecy might I glean if I listened closely enough?

The weight of destiny pressed down upon us all, but I couldn't shake the feeling that we were merely pawns in a game far greater than we could comprehend. And as I looked at Kael's too-bright smile, I wondered just how much he truly knew about the darkness that threatened to consume us all.

A whisper of movement caught my eye, and I turned to see a figure emerge from the gloom. Lyra Windwhisper glided forward, her silver hair gleaming in the dim light like a beacon of hope. Or perhaps a portent of our doom.

She nodded to us, her blue eyes piercing through the murk. "Welcome, travelers," she intoned, her voice as soft as a spring breeze yet laden with unspoken power. "I trust your journey was... uneventful?"

I suppressed a shudder, remembering the horrors we'd faced on the road. "As uneventful as one might expect, given the circumstances," I replied, my tone carefully neutral.

Lyra's gaze lingered on me, and I felt as though she could see right through my facade, peering into the darkest corners of my soul. What secrets might she uncover there? What sins might she judge?

"Your dedication to the cause is admirable," she said at last, her words falling like droplets of ice upon my fevered mind. "But I wonder, are you truly prepared for what lies ahead?"

Before I could formulate a response, the air around us seemed to thicken, charged with an ancient energy that made the hairs on the back of my neck stand on end. Eldran Silveroak materialized before us, his weathered face a map of countless years and untold sorrows.

"The path you walk is treacherous," he intoned, his voice resonating with the weight of ages. "But it is not without hope."

I found myself leaning forward, drawn in by the promise of wisdom. But as Eldran's eyes met mine, I recoiled. For in their depths, I saw not comfort but a reflection of my own haunted past magnified a thousandfold.

"Tell us, wise one," I heard myself say, my voice barely more than a whisper. "What hope can there be in a world consumed by darkness?"

Eldran's lips curved into a smile that held no mirth. "Hope, dear child, is but the first step on the road to disappointment."

As Eldran's words hung in the air like a funeral dirge, a soft radiance began to permeate the room. I turned, my eyes drawn to the source of this ethereal glow. High Priestess Althea Light-bringer approached her every movement a study in grace. Her presence seemed to push back the shadows that clung to the edges of my vision, but I couldn't shake the feeling that those same shadows now coiled tighter around my heart.

"My children," she spoke, her melodic voice a balm to my troubled soul. "Though the path before us is fraught with peril, we must not lose faith."

I wanted to believe her, to let her soothing words wash away my doubts. But the cynic in me whispered that faith was a luxury I could ill afford.

"And what of those whose faith has long since abandoned them, High Priestess?" I asked, my voice rough with bitterness.

Althea's eyes met mine, and for a moment, I felt laid bare before her. "Even the faithless have a role to play in the grand tapestry of fate," she replied, her words carrying the weight of ancient prophecies.

As if summoned by some unspoken command, a figure emerged from the gathered group. General Darius Ironheart stood at rigid attention, his battle-scarred visage a stark contrast to Althea's serene countenance.

"Words and faith are well and good," he declared, his voice cutting through the air like a blade, "but it is steel and blood that will win this war."

I felt a chill run down my spine at his words. How many times had I heard such declarations? How many times had they led to nothing but death and regret?

"And what of the cost, General?" I found myself asking. "How many more must fall before we claim victory?"

Darius fixed me with a steely gaze. "As many as necessary," he replied without hesitation. "I will lead the charge myself if that's what it takes to stem this demonic tide."

I nodded, admiring his resolve even as I pitied it, for I knew all too well the price of such unwavering commitment. It was etched into my very soul, a constant reminder of the mistakes that had led me to this moment.

As the weight of Darius's words settled upon us, the shadows in the corner of the room seemed to deepen, coalescing into a form both alluring and unsettling. I felt my breath catch in my throat as Vesper Nocturne materialized, their presence a void that threatened to consume all light.

"The tide ebbs and flows, but the abyss remains constant," Vesper intoned, their voice a whisper that echoed in the chambers of my mind. "What lies beneath may yet be our salvation... or our undoing."

I struggled to decipher their cryptic utterance, my thoughts a maelstrom of possibilities and dangers. Was Vesper an ally or a harbinger of our doom?

Before I could voice my concerns, a shimmer of starlight caught my eye. Selene Starfire glided into our midst, her luminescent skin casting a soft glow that seemed to push back the encroaching darkness.

"The cosmos speaks of great change," Selene said, her eyes swirling with celestial knowledge. "We stand at the precipice of destiny, where choices made in shadow will shape the fate of worlds."

I felt a tremor of recognition at her words, a memory of ancient lore I had long ago forsaken. "And what of those who have already fallen from grace?" I asked, my voice barely above a whisper. "Is there redemption in this cosmic design?"

Selene's gaze met mine, and for a moment, I saw the vastness of eternity reflected in her eyes. "Even the darkest star has its place in the heavens," she replied her words a balm to my tormented soul.

But as I looked around at our assembled group, I couldn't help but wonder: would our combined light be enough to pierce the coming darkness, or were we merely delaying the inevitable fall?

I took a deep breath, the weight of our purpose settling heavily upon my shoulders. The air around us crackled with tension, thick with unspoken fears and hidden agendas. It was time to reveal the full extent of our predicament.

"My friends," I began, my voice cutting through the silence like a blade, "we stand on the precipice of annihilation." The words tasted bitter on my tongue, each syllable a reminder of my own failures. "The demonic forces grow stronger with each passing moment, their tendrils of corruption seeping into the very fabric of our world."

I could feel their eyes upon me, probing, questioning. Did they sense the tremor in my voice, the guilt that gnawed at my core? I pressed on, determined to convey the urgency of our situation.

"We must act now before the last vestiges of hope are extinguished. Our alliance may be fragile, but it is all that stands between us and oblivion."

As I spoke, I watched their faces, searching for signs of doubt or resolve. Kael's usual smirk had faded, replaced by a grim set to his jaw. Lyra's eyes darted between us all, calculating, assessing.

Eldran stood as still as an ancient oak, his weathered face betraying nothing.

The silence that followed my words was deafening. I could almost hear the gears turning in their minds, weighing the risks against the potential rewards. The air grew thick with unspoken questions and simmering tensions.

"And what of our own demons?" Vesper's whisper slithered through the gathering, a serpent of doubt. "Can we trust ourselves, let alone each other?"

I felt a chill run down my spine. How much did Vesper know of my past transgressions? Of the choices that had led us to this moment? I pushed the thoughts aside, focusing on the task at hand.

"Trust is a luxury we cannot afford," I replied, my voice steadier than I felt. "But unity in purpose must suffice. The fate of all hangs in the balance."

As I scanned the faces of our newfound allies, I saw a kaleidoscope of emotions: determination, fear, suspicion, hope. Would it be enough to forge an alliance strong enough to face the coming storm? Or would our own darkness tear us apart before we even began?

As the weight of our grim reality settled upon us like a funeral shroud, Kael's voice suddenly cut through the silence, sharp and irreverent.

"Well, at least we've got a diverse group of misfits to face the apocalypse," he quipped, his stormy eyes glinting with mischief. "I've always wanted to be part of a doomed suicide mission."

I caught Lyra's gaze, expecting her usual stoic disapproval. To my surprise, a reluctant smile tugged at the corners of her mouth, a fleeting ray of moonlight in our somber gathering. For a moment, the suffocating tension eased, and I glimpsed a flicker of camaraderie that might—just might—see us through the horrors to come.

But the reprieve was short-lived. Eldran stepped forward, his silver beard catching the dim light, reminding me of starlight on a river of time. When he spoke, his voice carried the weight of centuries.

"Our path is treacherous but not without hope," he intoned, his eyes sweeping across our ragtag band. "We must strike at the heart of the demon's power, severing its connection to our world."

As Eldran outlined his strategy, I found myself nodding along, even as a part of me recoiled at the audacity of his plan. It was madness, surely. And yet, what choice did we have?

"The ritual will require sacrifice," Eldran continued, his words falling like stones into a still pond. "Each of us must be prepared to give all."

I watched as understanding dawned on the faces around me. Some, like Darius, set their jaws with grim determination. Others, like Vesper, seemed to retreat further into the shadows. And me? I felt the familiar icy tendrils of dread coiling around my heart. What more could I possibly give when I'd already lost so much?

But I knew, deep in the marrow of my bones, that I would give it all again if it meant a chance at redemption. For in the face of annihilation, what were my personal demons but pale shadows of the true horror that awaited us all?

As the weight of Eldran's words settled upon us, a gentle radiance began to fill the room. High Priestess Althea stepped forward, her golden hair seeming to catch and hold the dim light. Her eyes, shimmering with an otherworldly gleam, swept over our gathered faces.

"Friends," she began, her voice as soft and soothing as a lullaby, "our strength lies not only in arms and strategy but in the bonds we forge." She raised her hands, palms up.

Chapter 7

Exploration

The portal swallowed us whole. Its maw a swirling vortex of starlight and shadow. We tumbled through the ether, our senses reeling as reality twisted and warped around us.

Then, suddenly, we were there: the Ethereal Realm.

My eyes struggled to adjust to the overwhelming radiance that suffused every particle of air. Galaxies spun lazily overhead, their cosmic dance hypnotic and terrifying. A haunting melody drifted on the wind, its unearthly tones sending shivers down my spine.

"My God," Michael breathed beside me. His face was slack with awe, his eyes wide as he took in the impossible vista before us.

I shared his wonderment, yet a creeping dread coiled in my gut. This place was beautiful, yes, but also alien and wrong. We did not belong here.

Glancing at Thalia, I caught the knowing smile playing across her lips. Of course, she would be at ease here, the inscrutable seer. Sometimes, I wondered if she truly was human at all.

Our allies gasped in unison, their collective intake of breath a startling reminder that we were not alone. I had almost forgotten their presence, so lost was I in my own tumultuous thoughts.

As we stood frozen in stunned silence, a figure emerged from the shimmering light: Selene Starfire. Even here, in this realm of wonders, she stood apart - ethereal and luminous, yet somehow more solid and real than our surroundings.

She nodded in greeting, her eyes twin pools of swirling stardust. "Welcome," she intoned, her voice resonating with cosmic power.

I wanted to speak, to ask a thousand questions clamoring in my mind. But my tongue lay leaden in my mouth, paralyzed by awe and lingering terror.

What dark purpose had brought us to this place of light? And what sins would we commit here in our quest to save our world?

The Ethereal Realm's beauty could not mask the weight of our mission. As Selene's gaze met mine, I saw my own doubts reflected there.

We had come too far to turn back now. But, oh, how I longed for the familiar shadows of home.

Selene beckoned us forward, her movements liquid grace. We followed, our feet treading a path of shimmering light that seemed to flow beneath us like a river of starshine. Each step sent ripples of luminescence outward, a haunting echo of our passage.

"Your journey," Selene's voice whispered in my mind, "is a celestial waltz. Every choice is a pirouette between destiny and doom."

I shuddered, her words plucking at the strings of my deepest fears. "And if we misstep?" I asked, my voice hoarse.

A sad smile curved her lips. "Then the music ends, dear one, for all of us."

We walked in silence after that, the weight of her words pressing down upon us. The beauty around us now seemed a mocking façade, hiding untold horrors.

As we rounded a bend, a mountain of pure crystal rose before us, its jagged peaks tearing at the star-strewn sky. My breath caught in my throat, wonder and dread warring within me.

"There," Selene said, pointing to the summit. "The answers

you seek await. But be warned – knowledge always comes at a price."

I stared at the towering spires, my heart pounding. What terrible truths lurked at the peak? And were we prepared to pay the cost of learning them?

"We have no choice," I murmured, more to myself than to the others. "We've come too far to turn back now."

As we began our ascent, I couldn't shake the feeling that, with each step, we were climbing closer to our doom.

The air grew thick as we climbed, each breath a struggle against the cloying scent of ancient magic. It coated my tongue, tasting of stardust and forgotten dreams. My companions trudged beside me in silence, their faces etched with grim determination.

"Do you feel it?" I whispered to Michael, my voice barely audible over the whisper of cosmic winds. "The weight of what we're about to do?"

He nodded, his eyes haunted. "It's crushing me," he admitted. "What if we're not strong enough?"

I had no answer for him. The same doubts gnawed at my own heart, a festering wound of uncertainty.

Selene glided ahead, her ethereal form seemingly untouched by our mortal struggles. I envied her serenity, even as I resented it. How easy it must be to guide others to their fate when you stand apart from it all.

At last, we crested the summit. My breath caught in my throat as I beheld the scene before us. A circle of beings stood waiting, their forms shimmering with starlight. They were beautiful and terrible to behold, their eyes holding the wisdom of eons.

"The Keepers of the Cosmic Sanctuary," Selene intoned, her voice reverent. "Guardians of the knowledge you seek."

I stepped forward, my heart pounding. What terrible secrets would they reveal? And would we survive the knowing?

The Keepers' voices filled my mind, a haunting melody that resonated through my very soul. I shuddered, feeling exposed as if they could see every dark corner of my being.

"Jessica," they sang in unison, their words both within and without. "Michael, you seek the return of dragons."

I nodded, unable to speak. Beside me, Michael tensed, his hand finding mine in a grip that bordered on painful.

"There is a way," the Keepers continued, their forms undulating like starlight on water. "An ancient ritual, a dance of elements that can bridge the void between worlds."

My heart leaped, even as dread coiled in my stomach. "What must we do?" I asked, my voice hoarse.

The air shimmered, and suddenly, I saw it - a vision of swirling energies, cosmic forces intertwining in a delicate balance. It was beautiful and terrifying, a dance on the edge of chaos.

"Precise," Michael murmured, his eyes wide. "So precise."

I understood then the enormity of what lay before us. One misstep, one moment of imbalance, and we could tear reality asunder. The weight of it threatened to crush me.

"Can we do this?" I whispered, more to myself than to anyone else. "Are we worthy of such power?"

The Keepers' voices echoed in my mind, neither reassuring nor condemning. "That," they intoned, "is for you to decide."

Selene's luminescent form glided forward, her eyes swirling with nebulae. "The dance is intricate," she murmured, her voice like stardust on the wind. "Each of you is a thread in the cosmic tapestry."

I swallowed hard, tasting ash. "And if we falter?"

"Then all is lost," Selene replied her words a dagger to my already fragile resolve.

She began to move, her body flowing like liquid starlight. "Watch," she commanded. "Feel the rhythm of the universe."

I tried to follow, my clumsy steps a mockery of her grace. Beside me, Michael stumbled, his face a mask of concentration.

"No," Selene chided gently. "You mustn't force it. Let the cosmos guide you."

"How?" I snapped, frustration bubbling up like tar in my chest. "We're not... we're just..."

"Mortal?" Selene finished, a sad smile playing on her lips. "Perhaps that is your strength."

She took my hand, her touch sending shivers down my spine. "Close your eyes, Jessica. Listen to the song of the stars."

I obeyed, darkness enveloping me. At first, there was nothing. Then, slowly, I began to hear it - a faint melody, achingly beautiful and terribly sad.

"I hear it," I whispered, tears pricking at my eyes.

"Now move," Selene instructed. "Let the music flow through you."

And suddenly, I was dancing. My body knew the steps, even if my mind did not. I felt Michael beside me, our movements in perfect sync.

As we danced, hope blossomed in my chest, fragile and painful. Could we truly bring the dragons back? And if we did, would it be our salvation... or our doom?

The dance ended, leaving me breathless and dizzy. As I opened my eyes, the celestial beings surrounding us began to glow, their forms pulsing with an otherworldly light. A wave of energy washed over me, filling every fiber of my being with a strength I'd never known.

"What's happening?" I gasped, my voice barely above a whisper.

Selene's eyes met mine, swirling with nebulae. "They offer their blessing, Jessica. A gift to aid you in the trials ahead."

The surge of power was intoxicating and seductive. I felt invincible, immortal. Yet beneath it all lurked a shadow of doubt, a gnawing fear that this newfound strength would corrupt us as it had so many before.

"Remember," Selene's voice cut through my thoughts, "we will be watching: silent guardians in your darkest hours."

Her words should have been comforting, but they sent a chill down my spine. How much would they see? How much would they judge?

As the glow faded, reality crashed back upon us. The weight of our mission settled on my shoulders like a shroud.

"It's time," Michael murmured beside me, his face etched with a determination I envied.

Selene nodded, her form already beginning to fade. "May the stars light your path," she whispered, her voice a haunting melody that echoed long after she had vanished.

We stood alone now, at the precipice of a journey that could save our world... or doom it entirely. And as we prepared to leave this realm of starlight and dreams, I couldn't shake the feeling that we were walking willingly into our own destruction.

The portal flickered, a maw of swirling darkness. I stepped through first, Michael close behind. The ethereal glow that had enveloped us moments ago vanished, replaced by the oppressive shadows of our own world. The transition was jarring, like plunging from a dream into a nightmare.

We stood together, our small group united by the weight of forbidden knowledge. The others' faces were ashen, mirroring the dread that gnawed at my insides.

"So this is it," I whispered, my voice sounding hollow in the gloom. "We hold the key to summoning dragons."

Michael's hand found mine, his grip firm but trembling slightly. "The fate of Earth," he murmured, his blue eyes meeting mine with an intensity that both comforted and unnerved me.

I forced a smile, though it felt more like a grimace. "No pressure, right?"

A humorless chuckle escaped his lips. "None at all."

We gazed at each other, a silent understanding passing between us. The enormity of our task threatened to crush us, yet we stood tall. What choice did we have?

"We're ready," I said, trying to infuse my words with a confidence I didn't feel. "Whatever trials lie ahead, we'll face them."

But as we turned to face the long road before us, I couldn't shake the nagging doubt. Were we truly prepared for what was to come? Or had we just sealed our own doom – and perhaps that of the entire world?

The path ahead stretched into darkness, a ribbon of shadow twisting through a land that suddenly felt alien and hostile. Each step echoed with the weight of our newfound purpose, the whispers of the Ethereal Realm still clinging to us like gossamer threads.

"I can't shake the feeling we're being watched," Lyra murmured, her silver hair catching what little light remained. Her eyes darted to the shadows, fingers twitching near her bow.

I swallowed hard, tasting the bitterness of fear. "Perhaps we are," I replied, my voice barely above a whisper. "By friend or foe, who can say?"

Kael's laugh cut through the gloom, sharp and brittle. "Oh, come now. Surely our newfound cosmic enlightenment should shield us from mundane terrors?"

His sarcasm did little to ease the chill that had settled in my bones. I wanted to believe in the hope we'd been given, in the promise of dragons returning to save us all. But hope, I'd learned, could be the cruelest deceiver.

"The ritual," I found myself saying, the words spilling out unbidden. "What if we can't... what if I can't..."

Azhara's hand on my shoulder silenced me, her touch both comforting and unsettling. "Doubt is the poison that will undo us all," she said, her voice carrying that eerie, melodic quality that made my skin prickle. "We must believe, or all is lost before we begin."

I nodded, not trusting myself to speak. We pressed on, the echoes of the Ethereal Realm fading with each step, replaced by the oppressive silence of our own world. The journey stretched before us, endless and daunting, but we carried within us a flicker of possibility – a dangerous, beautiful thing that could either save us or consume us entirely.

CHAPTER 8

RISING TENSION

Heavy dew dripped from gnarled branches as we crept through the shadowy forest, our breaths misting in the frigid air. I clutched my staff tighter; its familiar weight was my only comfort in this oppressive gloom.

"Stay alert," I whispered, my voice barely audible over the pounding of my heart. "We're not alone here."

Michael nodded grimly, his eyes scanning the twisted trees looming on all sides. The others fanned out behind us, their faces pale smudges in the murk.

How long had we been wandering these cursed woods? Hours? Days? Time seemed to blur here, reality bending under the weight of ancient magic. With each step, memories of warmth and light felt more distant, like fading dreams.

A twig snapped somewhere to our left. We froze, straining to hear.

"Did you—" Thalia began, but I silenced her with a sharp gesture.

There—a rustling in the underbrush, drawing nearer. My pulse quickened as I raised my staff, its crystal tip glowing faintly. Around me, my companions readied their own implements of power.

"Steady," Michael murmured. "Remember your training."

Training. As if nothing could have prepared us for this nightmare. I wanted to laugh, or perhaps to weep. Instead, I gritted my teeth and focused on the writhing shadows before us.

The rustling grew louder, branches snapping as something large pushed through the foliage. I could hear ragged breathing—or was that simply the wind? My palms grew slick with sweat as I struggled to maintain my grip.

"Jessica," Michael said softly. "Whatever happens, we face it together."

I nodded, not trusting my voice. Together. The word echoed in my mind, a feeble shield against the horrors that awaited us. As the creature drew ever closer, I wondered which of us would be the first to fall.

The creature burst forth, a grotesque fusion of shadow and flame that seemed to devour the very light around it. Its form writhed and pulsed, defying natural law.

"Now!" I shouted, my voice cracking with fear and determination.

We moved as one, a symphony of arcane energies erupting from our fingertips. Selene's celestial fire blazed forth, searing the air with starlight. Beside her, Vesper's shadows danced and coiled, their voices a haunting whisper as they wove their enigmatic spells.

My own magic felt weak in comparison, a feeble spark against the encroaching darkness. Still, I poured every ounce of my being into the incantation, praying it would be enough.

The creature reeled under our assault, its flesh—if such a thing could be called flesh—bubbling and hissing. For a moment, hope flared in my chest.

Then it struck back.

A wave of pure malevolence slammed into us, scattering our formation like leaves in a gale. I stumbled across the forest floor, my breath knocked from my lungs. Gasping, I scrambled to my feet, searching desperately for my companions.

　　　　　　　　　　　

"Michael!" I called out, my voice barely audible over the creature's unholy roar. "Selene!"

Through the chaos, I caught a glimpse of Vesper, their form seeming to melt into the very shadows as they dodged the creature's attacks. Their eyes met mine for a fleeting instant, and I shivered at the unfathomable depths I saw there.

"Regroup!" Michael's voice cut through the din. "We can't let it divide us!"

I staggered toward his voice, my heart pounding a frantic rhythm against my ribs. How long could we hold out against such relentless fury? And what darker horrors awaited us beyond this forest of nightmares?

The creature's baleful eyes locked onto me, and in that moment, my courage faltered. Doubt gnawed at my resolve, whispering insidious thoughts. What if we weren't strong enough? What if our quest was doomed from the start?

"Jessica, watch out!" Michael's warning pierced through my spiral of fear.

I dove to the side, narrowly avoiding a tendril of shadow that lashed where I'd stood. Rolling to my feet, I gritted my teeth. No, I couldn't give in to despair. Not now. Not when so much hung in the balance.

"We've got this," I muttered, more to myself than to anyone else. "Remember why we're here."

Images flashed through my mind: the villages ravaged by darkness, the faces of those counting on us. I drew strength from them, from the trust they had placed in us, and from the unwavering determination I saw in Michael's eyes as he stood his ground against the monstrosity.

"Michael!" I called out. "Can you see any weak points?"

He nodded, his lanky frame taut with concentration. "There! Where the shadows meet the flame. If we hit it together—"

"Got it," I interrupted, already gathering my magic. The familiar tingle of power coursed through my veins, steadying my nerves.

As one, we unleashed our spells. Mine was a bolt of pure, searing light; Michael's was a cascading wave of frost. The conflicting energies collided with the creature's form, tearing at its very essence.

It shrieked a sound that set my teeth on edge and sent shivers down my spine. But I could see it weakening, its movements growing sluggish.

"Now, Michael!" I yelled. "Finish it!"

He didn't hesitate. With a grace I'd never seen in him before, Michael leapt forward, his hands weaving an intricate pattern in the air. The words he spoke were ancient and powerful, each syllable resonating with otherworldly energy.

The creature writhed, caught in the grip of Michael's spell. Its form began to unravel, wisps of shadow and flame dissipating into the night air like smoke.

With a final, gut-wrenching wail, it collapsed in on itself, leaving nothing but an echoing silence and the acrid scent of spent magic.

I stared at the empty space where the monster had been, my breath coming in ragged gasps. "We... we did it," I whispered, scarcely believing it myself.

I sank to my knees, the adrenaline ebbing away and leaving me shaky. Around me, the others were in similar states of exhaustion. Thalia leaned heavily against a gnarled tree, her usually pristine robes singed and torn. Elias slumped to the forest floor, his chest heaving.

Michael stumbled toward me, his face pale and drawn. He reached for my hand, and I felt his fingers tremble as they interlaced with mine. "You alright?" he murmured.

I nodded, not trusting my voice. The relief was palpable but fleeting. Already, the shadows seemed to deepen around us as if the forest itself were closing in.

"We can't stay here," Elias said, breaking the momentary silence. His voice was hoarse, tinged with urgency. "That thing... it won't be the last."

"Agreed," Thalia chimed in, pushing herself upright. "But where do we go from here? The path to the Ethereal Realm—"

"We don't even know if it exists!" I snapped, immediately regretting my outburst. The others turned to me, their expressions a mix of surprise and concern.

Michael squeezed my hand gently. "Jess..."

I pulled away, suddenly restless. "I'm sorry, it's just... we're chasing legends and myths while real monsters are tearing our world apart. What if we're wrong? What if the dragons can't help us?"

The silence that followed was heavy, charged with unspoken fears. I could see the doubt flickering in their eyes, mirroring my own. We'd come so far and risked so much, but the weight of our mission seemed to grow with each passing moment.

Thalia was the first to speak. "We have to believe," she said softly, her voice carrying a conviction I envied. "The alternative is... unthinkable."

I wanted to argue, to give voice to the gnawing doubts that plagued me. But as I looked at their faces—tired, scared, but still determined—I swallowed my words. They needed hope, even if I couldn't feel it myself.

"You're right," I conceded, forcing a smile that felt brittle on my lips. "We press on. But we need a plan, a real one. No more stumbling through the dark."

As we huddled together, plotting our next move, I couldn't shake the feeling that we were merely delaying the inevitable. The darkness was growing, and I feared our light might not be enough to hold it back.

I led our somber procession deeper into the forest, each step feeling heavier than the last. The trees loomed ever closer, their gnarled branches reaching out like skeletal fingers, ready to snatch us from the narrow path. Shadows danced at the edge of my vision, taunting me with glimpses of horrors I dared not name.

"Does anyone else feel like the forest is... watching us?" Kael whispered, his usual wit subdued by the oppressive atmosphere.

I nodded, not trusting my voice. The air grew thick and cloying as if the very essence of dread had seeped into our surroundings. My skin crawled with each breath, and I found myself straining to hear beyond the muffled crunch of our footsteps.

Lyra's voice cut through the silence, taut with tension. "Movement, ahead and to the left."

Before I could respond, the shadows erupted into a frenzy of teeth and claws. Demonic entities, more numerous than before, poured from the darkness like a tide of nightmares made flesh.

"Formation!" I shouted, my body moving on instinct as I raised my hands, arcane energy crackling at my fingertips.

We fell into a practiced rhythm, a deadly dance we'd perfected through too many battles. Azhara's blade sang as it cleaved through the air, each strike precise and devastating. Kael's spells lit up the gloom, brief flashes of brilliance that seared my eyes and sent the demons reeling.

As I unleashed a torrent of fire, incinerating a cluster of writhing shadows, a chilling thought crept into my mind. How long could we keep this up? How many more waves of darkness could we repel before one of us faltered?

"On your left, Jess!" Lyra's warning came just in time. I spun, narrowly avoiding a set of razor-sharp claws that would have opened my throat.

The battle raged on, a symphony of chaos and desperation. With each demon we felled, two more seemed to take its place. Doubt gnawed at me, threatening to overwhelm my resolve. What if this was how it ended? Not in some grand confrontation, but here in this nameless forest, worn down by an endless tide of lesser evils?

No. I couldn't let that thought take root. We had come too far and sacrificed too much. As another wave of demons surged forward, I dug deep, drawing on reserves of strength I didn't know I possessed.

"Hold the line!" I roared, my voice carrying over the din of battle. "We are not dying here!"

Amidst the chaos, I caught a glimpse of Thalia. She stood apart, her silver hair gleaming in the darkness, her violet eyes fixed on some distant point beyond the battle. Even as demonic claws raked the air inches from her face, she remained still, untouched.

"Thalia!" I cried out, fear gripping my heart. "What are you—"

But my words were cut short as another wave of shadows crashed against us. I lost sight of her, consumed by the desperate struggle to stay alive.

Time lost all meaning. We fought, bled, and fought some more. The forest itself seemed to close in around us, the trees looming like silent spectators to our torment.

When I next saw Thalia, her lips were moving in a silent chant, her hands tracing intricate patterns in the air. A faint shimmer surrounded her, growing stronger with each passing moment.

"The dragons," she whispered, her voice carrying to me despite the cacophony of battle. "I can see them, Jessica. So beautiful, so distant. They're waiting for us."

I parried a demon's strike, my arms aching with fatigue. "That's great, Thalia, but we could use some help here and now!"

She turned to me, her eyes filled with a mixture of sorrow and determination. "We must endure. This is but a taste of what's to come. The dragons... they're our only hope against the true darkness."

As if to punctuate her words, a massive shadow erupted from the ground, towering over us. Its roar shook the very air, and I felt my resolve wavering.

But Thalia's words echoed in my mind. The dragons. Our hope. Our mission.

With a defiant cry, I raised my weapon once more, ready to face whatever horrors the night had in store for us.

The battle's aftermath left us battered and drained. I slumped against a gnarled tree trunk, my breath ragged, every muscle screaming in protest. Michael knelt beside me, his face a mask of concern as he examined a gash on my arm.

"It's not as bad as it looks," I lied, wincing as he applied pressure.

"We're running low on healing herbs," he murmured, his blue eyes clouded with worry. "And our rations..."

I nodded, the weight of our situation settling like lead in my stomach. "Time's slipping away from us, isn't it?" I whispered.

Michael's hand found mine, squeezing gently. "We'll make it, Jess. We have to."

Across the clearing, Thalia tended to the others, her movements sluggish with exhaustion. The urgency of our quest pressed down on us all, an invisible weight threatening to crush our spirits.

"The dragons," I muttered, more to myself than Michael. "We need to reach them before..."

My words trailed off as the forest around us began to thin, giving way to a barren landscape that sent a chill down my spine. Gone were the shadowy trees, replaced by jagged rocks and withered vegetation. The air grew thick and heavy with an unnatural cold that seeped into my bones.

"This isn't right," Michael said, his voice low and tense. "It's as if the land itself is dying."

I struggled to my feet, my eyes scanning the desolate horizon. "Or being consumed," I added, unable to shake the feeling that we were walking into the maw of some great, hungry beast.

The others gathered around us, their faces etched with a mixture of fear and determination. We'd come too far to turn back now, but the path ahead promised only greater peril.

"We press on," I declared, my voice steadier than I felt. "Whatever comes, we face it together."

As we set out across the blighted terrain, I couldn't help but wonder if we were already too late. The dragons seemed further away than ever, their promise of salvation fading like a dream upon waking. But I pushed those doubts aside, focusing on each step, each breath. We had no choice but to continue, to believe that our efforts would not be in vain.

The chill air nipped at our skin, a constant reminder of the growing darkness that threatened to engulf us all.

I cast a furtive glance at my companions, their faces drawn and haggard in the fading light. Lyra's silver hair, once luminous, now seemed dull and lifeless. Kael's usual smirk had vanished, replaced by a tight-lipped grimace. Even Azhara's normally commanding presence felt diminished as if the very land were leeching away our strength.

"We should make camp soon," I murmured, my voice barely above a whisper. "Before the darkness swallows us whole."

Michael nodded, his eyes never leaving the horizon. "But where? This wasteland offers no shelter, no comfort."

A bitter laugh escaped my lips. "Comfort? We left that behind long ago, my friend."

As we trudged on, the silence grew oppressive, broken only by the crunch of our footsteps on the barren earth. My mind wandered to darker places, to the sins that had led us here. How many had suffered for our choices? How many more would pay the price if we failed?

"Jessica," Azhara's voice cut through my brooding. "What do you see?"

I squinted into the distance, where the land seemed to blur and shift. "I'm not sure. It's as if... as if the world is unraveling at the seams."

A cold dread settled in my stomach. We were nearing the edge of reality itself, and beyond lay only chaos and madness. The true test of our resolve awaited us there, in that formless void where even dragons feared to tread.

"We'll face it together," I said, echoing my earlier words, though they rang hollow now. "Whatever comes."

But as night fell and we huddled together against the encroaching darkness, I couldn't shake the feeling that we were merely delaying the inevitable. The dragons, our last hope, seemed further away than ever, and the weight of our mission threatened to crush us all.

CHAPTER 9

BACKSTORY

The flickering candlelight danced across Thalia Moonshadow's face, her violet eyes seeming to hold the weight of centuries within their depths. I couldn't look away, entranced by her otherworldly presence, as she stood before Michael and me in the cramped, shadowy room. The silence stretched, thick and oppressive, until I thought I might suffocate beneath it.

When Thalia finally spoke, her soft voice carried the cadence of forgotten melodies. "There are truths," she began, "that lie hidden in the spaces between worlds, in the whispers of dying stars."

I shivered, though, whether from her words or the chill that perpetually clung to this place, I couldn't say. What dark secrets was she about to unveil? And were we prepared to bear their weight?

"Long ago," Thalia continued, her gaze distant, "when the Earth was young, and magic flowed like rivers through the land, a pact was forged between the great dragons and a man who would become legend."

"Merlin," I breathed, the name escaping my lips unbidden.

Thalia's eyes snapped to mine, and I felt pinned beneath their intensity. "Yes," she murmured. "Merlin. A figure of such power that even now, centuries later, we tremble at the mention of his name."

Michael shifted beside me, his discomfort palpable. I knew he struggled to reconcile the fantastical elements of our quest with his rational mind. But even he couldn't deny the aura of ancient wisdom that cloaked Thalia like a second skin.

"The celestial dragons," Thalia said, her voice dropping to barely more than a whisper, "entrusted Merlin with a sacred duty – the protection of Earth itself."

My mind reeled at the implications. How could one man, no matter how powerful, bear such a monumental responsibility? And if Merlin had truly vanished, as the legends claimed, what did that mean for our world?

"But surely," I ventured, my voice sounding small and insignificant in the wake of Thalia's revelations, "there were others? Merlin couldn't have been alone in this task?"

A sad smile ghosted across Thalia's lips. "There were others, yes. But none who could match Merlin's mastery of the arcane, his connection to the very fabric of existence."

I closed my eyes, overwhelmed by the enormity of it all. The candles guttered, casting distorted shadows on the walls that seemed to writhe with a life of their own. When I opened my eyes again, Thalia was watching me with an expression I couldn't decipher.

"You carry a great burden," she said softly, and I wondered if she could see the guilt that gnawed at my soul, the sins of my past that haunted my every step. "But remember, even in the darkest night, hope endures."

Her words offered little comfort. For in that moment, surrounded by secrets and shadows, I feared that hope might be the most dangerous illusion of all.

As Thalia continued her tale, her hands began to move in slow, deliberate patterns. I watched, transfixed, as her flowing robes shimmered with celestial designs that seemed to dance and swirl in the flickering candlelight. Each gesture emphasized the weight of her words and the gravity of Merlin's cosmic role.

"Merlin's rise was not mere chance," she intoned her voice a haunting melody that sent shivers down my spine. "It was a culmination of power and destiny, intertwined."

I found myself leaning forward, drawn in by the rhythmic cadence of her speech. The room seemed to fade away, replaced by visions of a bygone era.

"How did he achieve such mastery?" I asked, my voice barely above a whisper.

Thalia's violet eyes met mine, filled with ancient sorrow. "Through sacrifice," she replied. "Through trials that would break lesser men. Merlin delved deep into the arcane arts, forging connections with cosmic forces beyond mortal comprehension."

As she spoke, I felt a chill creep into my bones. What terrible price had Merlin paid for his power? And what price might we yet pay for his absence?

"But surely," I protested weakly, "such power comes at a cost."

Thalia nodded, her silver hair catching the candlelight. "Indeed. And that cost..." She paused, her gaze distant. "That cost is still being paid."

I shuddered, unable to shake the feeling that we were standing on the precipice of something vast and terrifying. The shadows in the room seemed to deepen, and for a moment, I could have sworn I heard the faint echo of an otherworldly scream.

The air grew heavy, thick with unspoken dread. Thalia's voice dropped to a whisper, each word a leaden weight.

"The dragons," she breathed, "guardians of realms beyond mortal ken."

My mind reeled, trying to grasp the enormity of what she described. I saw them in flashes - scales gleaming like polished galaxies, wings that could eclipse the sun. Their eyes, ancient and terrible, bored into my soul.

"How... how big were they?" I stammered, my throat dry.

"Big enough to make mountains tremble," Thalia replied, her

gaze far away. "Their breath could ignite stars or freeze oceans. And yet..." She paused, a flicker of something - fear? Awe? - crossing her face. "And yet, they bowed to Merlin."

I shuddered, picturing these cosmic behemoths yielding to a single man. What kind of power must Merlin have wielded?

"But he's gone now, isn't he?" I whispered, dreading the answer.

Thalia's eyes met mine, filled with an unfathomable sadness. "Yes," she murmured. "Vanished without a trace."

The room seemed to darken, shadows creeping in at the edges of my vision. I felt a void opening up inside me, a yawning chasm of vulnerability.

"How?" I managed to croak.

"No one knows," Thalia said, her voice thick with melancholy. "One day, he simply... wasn't there anymore. And with him went our shield against the darkness."

I shivered, suddenly aware of how exposed we all were. Without Merlin, what hope did we have against the terrors that lurked beyond our world?

The weight of Thalia's words pressed down on me, crushing my chest. Her violet eyes, deep as the cosmos, seemed to peer into my very soul. I felt naked, exposed as if all my fears and inadequacies were laid bare before her ancient gaze.

"The magical community," she continued, her voice a haunting melody, "it's like a ship adrift in a storm without its captain. We're... lost."

I swallowed hard, trying to dislodge the lump in my throat. "Surely someone tried to find him?" I asked, desperation creeping into my voice.

Thalia's lips curled into a bitter smile. "Oh, they tried. So many tried."

She began to weave tales of brave witches and wizards who had ventured forth, seeking the lost warlock. Her words painted vivid pictures in my mind - a sorceress scaling treacherous, mist-shrouded peaks, a young mage delving into forgotten catacombs thick with ancient curses.

"What happened to them?" Michael whispered beside me, his face pale.

Thalia's eyes glittered in the candlelight. "Some returned, broken in body and spirit. Others... well, the silence speaks for itself."

I shuddered, imagining the fates of those who never came back. What horrors had they encountered? What dark forces now guarded Merlin's secrets?

"But surely," I began, my voice trembling, "surely there must be some hope?"

Thalia's gaze pierced me, and I felt the weight of centuries in that look. "Hope, dear one," she said softly, "can be the cruelest magic of all."

The silence stretched, a living thing that coiled around us, squeezing the breath from my lungs. Thalia's eyes, those deep violet pools of ancient knowledge, seemed to look through me, beyond me, to some distant point I couldn't fathom.

"And yet," she whispered, her voice barely audible, "hope persists."

My heart leaped, a traitorous surge of optimism I tried desperately to quash. I'd learned the hard way that hope often led to deeper despair.

"You mean..." Michael's voice cracked. "Merlin might still be alive?"

Thalia's lips curved into an enigmatic smile. "The threads of fate are not so easily severed, especially for one as... singular as Merlin."

I leaned forward, drawn in despite myself. "But how? After all this time?"

"Time," Thalia mused, her fingers tracing patterns in the air, leaving faint trails of silvery light, "is a fickle mistress to those who've tasted the deepest wells of magic."

She spoke of whispered prophecies, of visions glimpsed in

scrying pools and dream-trances. Her words painted tantalizing fragments: a staff crackling with cosmic energy, a whirlwind of autumn leaves concealing a figure of legend, the triumphant cry of a dragon echoing across barren lands suddenly bursting into bloom.

"The balance," Thalia intoned, her voice taking on a rhythmic cadence that seemed to resonate in my very bones, "teeters on a knife's edge. But the scales may yet be righted."

Hope bloomed in my chest, painful and exhilarating. I wanted to cling to it, to let it lift me from the mire of doubt I'd been drowning in. But the cynic in me, the part scarred by too many bitter disappointments, held back.

"And if these prophecies are wrong?" I asked, hating the tremor in my voice. "If we're chasing shadows and fairy tales?"

Thalia's gaze softened, and for a moment, I glimpsed a profound sadness behind her mystical façade. "Then we face the darkness with courage, knowing we dared to hope when all seemed lost."

I felt Michael tense beside me, his breath catching. Thalia's violet eyes locked onto us, twin pools of ancient wisdom that seemed to pierce through flesh and bone, peering into the very essence of our souls. Her aura pulsed, a shimmering veil that drew us inexorably closer to her world of enigmas and half-truths.

"The path ahead is treacherous," Thalia murmured her voice a melodic whisper that sent chills down my spine. "But you carry within you the embers of a greater destiny."

I wanted to scoff, to dismiss her words as the flowery nonsense of a charlatan. Yet something in her gaze held me captive, a gravitational pull I couldn't explain or resist.

"What does that even mean?" I croaked, my throat suddenly dry.

Thalia's lips curved in a smile that didn't quite reach her eyes. "It means, dear Jessica, that the threads of fate have begun to tighten. You stand at a crossroads, and your choices will echo through the tapestry of existence."

Michael leaned forward, his voice barely above a whisper. "How can we possibly—"

But Thalia raised a hand, silencing him. She closed her eyes, swaying slightly as if caught in an otherworldly breeze. When she spoke again, her words carried a weight that seemed to bend the very air around us.

"Listen closely, seekers of the lost," she intoned. "When starlight kisses the ancient stones and shadows whisper forgotten names, seek the place where two worlds bleed. There, in the twilight between realms, you'll find the key that unlocks the door to Merlin's fate."

The candles flickered, casting grotesque shadows on the walls. As Thalia's words faded, I felt a surge of determination tinged with a creeping dread. What horrors lay ahead on this quest? What price would we pay for answers?

Yet, as I met Michael's gaze, I saw my own resolve mirrored there. Whatever awaited us, we would face it together.

CHAPTER 10

MIDPOINT REVEAL

The flickering candlelight cast long shadows across the chamber, dancing over the faces of my companions as we hunched over crumbling tomes and ancient artifacts. The air hung heavy with the musty scent of forgotten knowledge and the faint hum of arcane energy that seemed to pulse through the very stones beneath our feet. I rubbed my bleary eyes, fighting against the fatigue that threatened to overwhelm me.

"Anything yet?" I asked, my voice barely above a whisper.

Michael shook his head, frustration etched in the lines of his face. "Nothing. These texts are as cryptic as ever."

I turned my attention back to the scroll before me, the spidery script swimming before my eyes. The words seemed to mock me, holding their secrets just out of reach. A chill ran down my spine, a familiar sense of dread creeping in. What dark truths lay hidden within these weathered pages?

Suddenly, a sharp gasp cut through the oppressive silence. My head snapped up to see Thalia Moonshadow, her ethereal form rigid with tension. Her violet eyes were wide, fixed upon the text before her.

"Thalia?" I whispered, almost afraid to break the spell that seemed to have fallen over her.

She looked up slowly, her face pale in the flickering light. When she spoke, her voice was barely audible, trembling with the weight of her discovery.

"I've found something," she breathed, her words laced with a mixture of awe and fear. "A passage... it speaks of a powerful warlock, trapped in a timeless void."

The air in the chamber seemed to grow colder, the shadows deeper. I felt my heart begin to race, a nameless dread clawing at my insides. What horrors had we unleashed with this revelation?

"A warlock?" Michael's voice was tight with tension. "Trapped in a void? What does it mean?"

Thalia's gaze seemed to look through us beyond the confines of our dim chamber. "It means," she said, her melodic voice taking on an almost hypnotic quality, "that our task is far greater and more perilous than we could have imagined."

I closed my eyes, fighting against the wave of despair that threatened to engulf me. How many more secrets lay buried in these ancient texts? How many more nightmares would we unearth before our quest was done?

As I opened my eyes, I caught a glimpse of my reflection in a polished silver artifact. For a moment, I barely recognized the haunted face staring back at me. What price would we pay for the knowledge we sought? And in the end, would it be worth the cost?

The silence that followed Thalia's words was deafening, broken only by the faint crackle of dying candles. I watched as the others exchanged tense glances, their faces a canvas of fear and uncertainty. The weight of the revelation settled upon us like a funeral shroud.

Michael's voice, barely above a whisper, cut through the oppressive silence. "Could it be... could the warlock be Merlin?" His words hung in the air, heavy with implication. "The legendary protector of Earth?"

I felt my breath catch in my throat. Merlin, the name itself, is a talisman of power and mystery. Could it truly be him, trapped in some nightmarish void beyond our comprehension?

Thalia's eyes, those deep violet pools of ancient wisdom, met Michael's gaze. She nodded solemnly, her silver hair shimmering in the dim light. "Yes," she breathed, her voice a haunting melody. "It is Merlin."

A collective shudder ran through our group. I felt it in my very bones, a chill that spoke of terrors yet to come.

"But how?" I found myself asking, my voice sounding foreign to my own ears. "How could one as powerful as Merlin be trapped?"

Thalia's gaze seemed to pierce through me, seeing the fear that lurked beneath my question. "A demon," she said, her words falling like leaden weights. "A demon of immense power is responsible for Merlin's imprisonment."

The revelation sent a shiver through us all. I felt it ripple through the room, a wave of dread that threatened to drown us in its depths. What manner of demon could imprison the legendary Merlin? And what hope did we have against such a foe?

My fists clenched involuntarily, nails biting into my palms. The pain grounded me, a sharp counterpoint to the maelstrom of thoughts whirling in my mind. Merlin, trapped. A demon of unimaginable power. Our world is teetering on the brink of annihilation.

"We must free him," I heard myself say, my voice raw with urgency. "Merlin's power... it's our only hope against the demonic forces."

The words hung in the air, heavy with the weight of destiny. I could feel the others' eyes upon me, their gazes a mix of fear and determination.

Michael stepped forward, his face a mask of grim resolve. "Jessica's right," he murmured. "But how do we even begin to locate a timeless void?"

The chamber fell silent, save for the faint whisper of ancient magic that seemed to pulse through the very stones. I looked around at our small band of allies, each face etched with the gravity of our situation.

Thalia's melodic voice broke the silence. "There are... ways," she said, her words slow and measured. "But they come at a great cost."

"What cost?" I demanded, my heart racing. "Whatever it is, we must pay it. The fate of our world hangs in the balance."

Eldran, his wizened face creased with worry, spoke up. "The paths to such places are treacherous, young one. They twist the mind and corrupt the soul. Are we prepared to risk everything?"

I felt a chill run down my spine at his words. Were we prepared? Could we bear the weight of such a burden? The faces of those I loved flashed before my eyes - my family, my friends, all those who would suffer if we failed.

"We have no choice," I whispered, more to myself than to the others. "The demon will not stop until our world is ashes. We must find Merlin, no matter the cost."

A heavy silence fell over the group, broken only by the soft rustling of ancient parchments. Each of us grappled with the enormity of the task ahead, our resolve tested by the looming specter of failure.

I watched as Kael Stoneforge's brow furrowed in concentration, his stormy eyes flickering with an intensity that belied his usual mischievous demeanor. The weight of our predicament seemed to press down upon him, aging him before my eyes.

"We must first locate the void," he said, his voice low and grave. "But tread carefully, my friends. The demon guarding Merlin's prison is no trifling matter."

A shiver ran through me at his words. What horrors awaited us in that timeless abyss? What nightmares would we face to free the legendary warlock?

"And how do you propose we find this void, Kael?" I asked, unable to keep the tremor from my voice.

Before he could answer, Lyra Windwhisper stepped forward,

her silver hair gleaming in the dim light. Her blue eyes blazed with a fierce determination that both inspired and terrified me.

"We combine our magic," she said, her melodic voice carrying an undercurrent of steel. "Our powers, united, might pierce the veil between worlds and lead us to Merlin's prison."

I saw nods of agreement ripple through our group, a flicker of hope igniting in their eyes. But doubt gnawed at my heart. Could we truly succeed where others had failed? Or were we doomed to join Merlin in that endless void, lost to time and memory?

As I gazed at my companions, I couldn't shake the feeling that we were teetering on the edge of an abyss, about to plunge into darkness from which there might be no return.

Eldran Silveroak cleared his throat, drawing our attention. His silver beard seemed to glow in the chamber's dim light, and his eyes were heavy with the weight of memory.

"Before we venture forth," he began, his voice a low rumble, "I must share a tale. In my youth, I encountered a void not unlike the one we seek."

A hush fell over us. Even the shadows seemed to lean in, eager to catch his words.

"It was a place of nightmares," Eldran continued, his gaze distant. "Reality bent and twisted. Time lost all meaning. I saw... things. Horrors that haunt me still."

I shuddered, my mind conjuring grotesque images. "How did you escape?" I whispered.

Eldran's eyes met mine, filled with a mixture of sorrow and steel. "Not all of us did."

Silence stretched between us, thick and oppressive. I swallowed hard, and my throat suddenly dried.

"We must be prepared for anything," Eldran warned. "The void will test us, body and soul."

With trembling hands, I reached for my pack. Around me, the others did the same, their movements slow and deliberate. The weight of our mission pressed down on us like a physical thing.

"What if we fail?" I murmured more to myself than to anyone else.

Michael's hand found my shoulder, his touch both comforting and terrifying. "Then the world falls to darkness," he said softly.

I nodded my heart a leaden weight in my chest. As we gathered our belongings, I couldn't shake the feeling that we were preparing for our own funeral.

The air grew heavy, suffocating. I felt the darkness pressing in, threatening to smother us all. But then, a gentle light began to emanate from High Priestess Althea Lightbringer. She stepped forward, her golden hair shimmering like a halo around her serene face.

"Let us pray," she intoned, her voice a melodic whisper that seemed to chase away the encroaching shadows.

We formed a circle, hands clasped tightly. I gripped Michael's hand on one side and Thalia's on the other, drawing strength from their warmth.

Althea's words washed over us, a soothing balm to our troubled souls. "Divine light, guide our path through the coming darkness. Shield us from the horrors that await, and grant us the strength to face our deepest fears."

As she spoke, I felt a curious warmth spreading through my chest. Was this hope? Or merely the last flicker of courage before it was extinguished forever?

"Bless our quest to free Merlin," Althea continued, her voice growing stronger. "May our resolve be unyielding, our hearts pure."

I closed my eyes, allowing her words to seep into my very being. For a moment, I could almost believe we might succeed.

The prayer ended, and silence fell once more. Slowly, reluctantly, we broke apart.

"It's time," I whispered, my voice hoarse.

We filed out of the chamber, our footsteps echoing ominously. The weight of our mission pressed down upon us, a crushing burden. As we stepped into the unknown, I couldn't shake the feeling that we were marching to our doom.

Yet we pressed on, our resolve hardened by Althea's prayer. Whatever horrors awaited us in the void, we would face them together.

The darkness swallowed us whole as we ventured deeper into the unknown. Each step felt heavier than the last as if the very air around us conspired to impede our progress. The shadows seemed to writhe and dance at the edges of my vision, taunting us with half-glimpsed terrors.

"Does anyone else feel like we're being watched?" Kael's whisper cut through the oppressive silence, his usual bravado noticeably absent.

I swallowed hard, fighting the urge to look over my shoulder. "It's just your imagination," I lied, my voice trembling slightly. But I felt it too—an unseen presence, malevolent and ancient, observing our every move.

Michael's hand found mine in the gloom, squeezing gently. I clung to that small comfort, even as doubts gnawed at the edges of my mind. Were we truly prepared for what lay ahead? Or had our hubris led us into a trap from which there was no escape?

As if sensing my unease, Vesper Nocturne materialized beside me, their form shifting and coalescing like smoke-given substance. "The path to greatness is often shrouded in darkness," they intoned, their voice a haunting whisper that seemed to come from everywhere and nowhere at once. "We must remain vigilant, lest we lose ourselves to the shadows that surround us."

I nodded, drawing strength from their pragmatic words. "You're right," I murmured. "We can't afford to let fear cloud our judgment, not when so much is at stake."

Vesper's eyes, black as the void itself, bore into mine. "Remember, Jessica, the greatest demons we face are often those within our own minds. Stay focused on our goal, and we may yet emerge victorious."

As we pressed onward, I clung to Vesper's advice like a lifeline.

Yet, with each step, the creeping horror of our task threatened to overwhelm me. The weight of our mission—to free Merlin and save our world—felt impossibly heavy. But I knew that to falter now would doom us all.

The darkness thickened around us, a living thing that seemed to pulse with malevolent intent. Our footsteps echoed in the oppressive silence and each sound a thunderclap that made my heart race. I could barely make out the silhouettes of my companions, their forms blurring and shifting in the gloom.

"Do you think Merlin knew?" I whispered to Michael, my voice trembling despite my efforts to steady it. "About the demon, the void... all of it?"

Michael's response was swallowed by the darkness, leaving me alone with my spiraling thoughts. The revelation of Merlin's fate gnawed at my insides, a constant reminder of the perilous path we tread.

"We're nearing the threshold," Thalia's voice floated back to us, tinged with both excitement and dread. "I can feel the void's energy pulsing ahead."

As we approached, the air grew heavy, charged with an other-worldly power that made my skin crawl. The darkness before us seemed to deepen, if such a thing were possible, into an absolute absence of light.

"This is it," I muttered, more to myself than to anyone else. "There's no turning back now."

With a collective intake of breath, our group stepped forward as one, allowing the unnatural darkness to swallow us whole. As we crossed that final threshold, I couldn't shake the feeling that we were walking willingly into the maw of some great cosmic beast.

The last thing I saw before the darkness consumed us entirely was the haunted look in my companions' eyes, a mirror of the terror and determination that warred within my own heart. Then, we were gone, vanished into the void, with only our fragile hope and the specter of Merlin's fate to guide us through the trials that lay ahead.

Chapter 11

Crisis Point

The ancient text mocked me as I paced the dim room, its cryptic symbols pulsing with eldritch power. My fingers trembled as I traced the arcane glyphs, each one a reminder of our folly. What had we awakened?

"Jessica, we need to focus," Michael's voice cut through my spiraling thoughts. "Panicking won't undo what's been done."

I whirled to face him, my voice sharp. "And what exactly have we done, Michael? Opened a gateway to some cosmic horror? Summoned an entity beyond our comprehension?"

He stood silhouetted against the window, the encroaching darkness outside mirroring the shadows that danced in his eyes. "We followed the ritual exactly as described. There's no way we could have known—"

"Known what?" I interrupted, my laugh bitter and hollow. "That meddling with forces beyond our understanding might have consequences? We should have known better."

Michael's jaw clenched, his guilt palpable in the heavy air between us. "We did this to save lives, Jessica. To protect our world from the demonic incursion. The ends justify—"

"Don't you dare finish that sentence," I hissed, my words dripping with venom. "We've no idea what we've truly unleashed."

As I resumed my frantic pacing, my mind raced with possibilities, each more terrifying than the last. The weight of our choices pressed down upon me, threatening to crush what little resolve remained.

Michael's gaze never left the window, as if he could somehow pierce the veil of night and glimpse our fate. His voice, when he finally spoke, was barely above a whisper. "We can't turn back now, Jessica. We're the only ones who can see this through."

I closed my eyes, willing the room to stop spinning. The scent of ancient magic hung heavy in the air, a constant reminder of the power we had foolishly tapped into. With each breath, I could feel it seeping into my very being, changing me in ways I couldn't begin to comprehend.

"And if we've damned ourselves in the process?" I asked, my voice small and fragile.

Michael turned to me then, his eyes haunted by the same fears that plagued my own thoughts. "Then we'll face that damnation together."

As we stood there, trapped in a prison of our own making, I couldn't shake the feeling that we were merely pawns in some cosmic game—a game whose rules we had yet to fully grasp.

A sudden stillness fell over the room, drawing my attention to Thalia. She sat motionless at the table, her eyes closed in deep meditation. The silver threads woven into her celestial robes shimmered faintly as if catching starlight from some unseen source. Her presence, usually a balm to my frayed nerves, now only served to heighten my unease.

"Can you feel it, Thalia?" I whispered, my voice cracking. "The discord... it's tearing us apart."

She didn't respond, but I saw the tension etched across her brow deepen. Even in her trance-like state, she couldn't escape the weight of our collective anguish.

The creak of the door startled me, and I whirled to see Kael and Lyra enter, their expressions as grave as death itself. My heart sank further. If even Kael's roguish charm had abandoned him, what hope did we have?

"Well?" I demanded, desperation clawing at my throat. "What news from the Ethereal Realm?"

Kael's storm-gray eyes met Lyra's piercing blue ones, a silent exchange that spoke volumes. When he finally turned to me, his usual wit was nowhere to be found. "The dragons... they're restless. The Cosmic Sanctuary trembles with their anticipation."

Lyra's melodic voice carried the weight of ancient sorrow as she added, "The stars themselves seem to dim in fear of what's to come."

I laughed then, a bitter, hollow sound that echoed in the oppressive silence. "And here we stand, mere mortals, daring to command such power. Have we learned nothing from our past follies?"

The room seemed to close in around me, shadows creeping at the edges of my vision. At that moment, I knew with terrifying certainty that our fates were sealed. We had set something in motion that could not be undone, and the price of our hubris would be steep indeed.

"Jessica," Michael's voice cut through my spiraling thoughts, firm yet tinged with an undercurrent of desperation. "We have no choice. The dragon-summoning ritual is our only hope."

I turned to face him, my chest tight with fear. "Our only hope? Or our final doom?" The words spilled from me like poison. "Have you forgotten the legends, Michael? The devastation wrought when mortals last dared to call upon such cosmic forces?"

His eyes, usually so steady, flickered with doubt. "I haven't forgotten," he said softly. "But Merlin—"

"Merlin is beyond our reach!" I cried, my voice cracking. "And we... we're not ready for this. The magic required, the consequences..."

Michael stepped closer, his face a mask of determination that couldn't quite hide the uncertainty beneath. "Rescuing Merlin is our only chance of turning the tide against the demonic hordes. You know this, Jessica. Without him, we're lost."

I laughed bitterly, the sound echoing in the oppressive silence. "And with him? We might be damned all the same."

As we stood there, locked in our impasse, I couldn't shake the feeling that we were puppets dancing on strings woven from our own past sins. The room seemed to darken, shadows creeping ever closer, whispering of the horrors that awaited us should we fail.

Or worse, should we succeed?

As the weight of our dilemma pressed down upon us, Thalia's voice cut through the gloom like a blade of moonlight. "We stand at a crossroads," she intoned, her violet eyes seeming to peer into realms unseen. "The path we choose will ripple across the tapestry of fate."

I turned to her, desperate for guidance, for some hint of what horrors or salvation lay ahead. But Thalia's face remained an inscrutable mask, her silver hair shimmering in the dim light like threads of destiny itself.

"The stakes," she continued, her words carrying the weight of prophecy, "are far greater than any one of us. We must consider not just our immediate goal but the consequences that will echo through time."

A chill ran down my spine. What terrors had she glimpsed in her visions? What price would we pay for our hubris?

As if summoned by Thalia's ominous words, the door creaked open. Eldran Silveroak entered, his silver beard catching the flickering candlelight, followed closely by High Priestess Althea Lightbringer. Their presence filled the room with an ancient power that made the air thick and heavy.

Eldran's eyes, sharp and knowing, swept over us. "I see the burden of choice weighs heavily upon you," he said, his voice deep and measured. "But remember, young ones, that even the mightiest tree must bend before the storm or risk being uprooted entirely."

Althea stepped forward, her golden hair seeming to glow with an inner light. "The path of righteousness is seldom easy," she said softly, her words a balm to my troubled soul. "But it is in our darkest moments that we must cling most fiercely to hope."

I wanted to believe her, to trust in the wisdom of these venerable figures. But the shadows of doubt clung to me like a second skin, whispering of past failures and future catastrophes.

The room crackled with tension, a palpable current of unease rippling through our once-united band. Kael's eyes flashed with defiance as he faced Jessica, his voice sharp as a blade.

"We can't afford to hesitate," he snapped. "Every moment we waste, Merlin's life hangs in the balance. Are you willing to sacrifice him for your fear?"

Jessica recoiled as if struck. "How dare you? I'm trying to protect us all from a fate worse than death!"

I watched, frozen, as the argument spiraled. Lyra's measured tones cut through the chaos, but even her usual calm seemed strained. "We must consider all angles. The ritual's power could tear the very fabric of reality."

My mind reeled, a tempest of conflicting thoughts. I'd led us here, hadn't I? To this precipice of disaster. Memories of past failures clawed at me – the village we couldn't save, the innocents lost to my reckless decisions.

"You don't understand," I heard myself say, my voice hollow. "The weight of those we've failed... it never leaves."

The room fell silent, all eyes upon me. At that moment, I felt naked and exposed. My guilt and my fears lay bare for all to see.

"Jessica," Thalia said softly, reaching for my hand. But I pulled away, the shadows of my past sins threatening to swallow me whole.

I turned away, unable to meet their gazes. The weight of leadership pressed down on me like a physical force, crushing the air from my lungs. My eyes fell on Michael, standing by the window, his broad shoulders tense. He spoke, his voice low and strained.

"We've come so far," he said, "but at what cost?" His fingers traced the weathered stone of the windowsill. "Every choice, every step... it's led us here. But what if there is the edge of an abyss?"

I watched him, my heart aching. Even Michael, my rock, was crumbling.

"We can't know," I whispered, more to myself than anyone. "That's the curse of leading, isn't it? Never knowing if we're walking toward salvation or damnation."

Michael turned, his eyes meeting mine. The warmth I usually found there was clouded by doubt. "And if it's damnation?" he asked. "If I lead you all to ruin?"

The question hung in the air, heavy and suffocating. No one dared answer.

Silence fell over us like a shroud. The room seemed to darken, shadows creeping in from the corners. Each of us retreated into our own minds, grappling with the enormity of what lay before us.

I closed my eyes, trying to shut out the world. But in the darkness, I saw only the faces of those we'd lost, those we might yet lose. Their whispers echoed in my skull, a cacophony of accusation and plea.

When I opened my eyes again, nothing had changed. We stood, united in our division, teetering on the precipice of a choice that could save or damn us all.

The silence shattered like glass.

"Enough," Vesper's voice cut through the gloom, a blade of shadow and starlight. They materialized from the darkness, their form fluid and ever-changing, eyes like pools of infinite night. "Your indecision is a noose tightening around all our necks."

I flinched. Their words were a slap across my face. Vesper's gaze swept over us, piercing and unforgiving.

"You speak of ruin," they continued, their voice echoing as if from another realm. "But what ruin awaits if we do nothing? The demons won't wait for your courage to solidify."

Michael stepped forward, his jaw clenched. "And if we fail? If we summon something we can't control?"

Vesper's laugh was cold, devoid of mirth. "Control is an illusion, Michael. We are all dancing on the edge of chaos."

Their words burrowed into my mind, awakening a terrible urgency. I looked around at my companions and saw the fear and determination warring in their eyes.

"We have to decide," I whispered, my voice trembling. "Now."

The air crackled with tension. We stood united yet divided, each of us wrestling with our own demons. The weight of the world pressed down upon us, a crushing, suffocating force.

As I gazed into the abyss of our future, I wondered: would our names be remembered as saviors or harbingers of doom?

The shadows seemed to deepen around us as if sensing our impending decision. I shivered, feeling the cold fingers of dread creep up my spine.

"We'll do it," I heard myself say, my voice sounding distant and unfamiliar. "We'll perform the ritual."

Kael's eyes locked with mine, storm-gray and filled with a mixture of relief and trepidation. "Jessica, are you certain?"

I nodded, trying to ignore the churning in my stomach. "We don't have a choice."

Lyra moved silently to the ancient text, her silver hair gleaming in the dim light. "Then we must prepare. The consequences of failure are... unthinkable."

As we began to gather the necessary components, I couldn't shake the feeling that we were sealing our own fates. The air grew thick with unspoken fears, each breath a struggle against the oppressive atmosphere.

"What if we're making a terrible mistake?" I whispered to Michael, my words barely audible.

He placed a hand on my shoulder, his touch meant to comfort but somehow only amplifying my unease. "We're out of options, Jess. This is our last hope."

I watched as Thalia traced arcane symbols on the floor, her usually serene face etched with worry. The candlelight flickered, casting monstrous shadows that danced on the walls, mocking our efforts.

With each passing moment, the weight of our decision bore down upon us. We were no longer just friends on an adventure – we had become harbingers of either salvation or destruction.

As we formed a circle around the glowing sigils, I caught a glimpse of my reflection in a nearby mirror. The person staring back was a stranger, eyes hollow with the knowledge of what we were about to unleash.

"May the gods forgive us," I murmured as we clasped hands and prepared to tear open the veil between worlds.

CHAPTER 12

ALL IS LOST

The candles flickered, casting long shadows across the ancient stone altar. My hand trembled as I gripped the silver athame, its weight suddenly oppressive. Beside me, Michael's face was a mask of grim determination.

"Are you ready?" he whispered, his voice barely audible over the ominous hum that filled the air.

I nodded, not trusting myself to speak. We had come too far to turn back now. The words of the incantation burned in my mind, a silent mantra I had repeated countless times: to free Merlin, to save the world. Noble goals that now felt hollow in the face of what we were about to attempt.

As we began to chant, the shadows seemed to deepen, writhing at the edges of my vision. A chill crept down my spine. Something was wrong.

"Jessica," Michael hissed. "Focus."

I tried to steady my voice, but each syllable felt like ash on my tongue. The knife grew heavier in my grasp. Memories of Merlin's legends flashed through my mind - his flowing silver beard, his cosmic staff. What right did we have to summon such power?

The shadows danced faster now, as if alive. Dread coiled in my stomach. "Michael, I don't think-"

"We can't stop," he cut me off, desperation in his eyes. "We're so close."

But close to what? As my voice faltered again, I couldn't shake the feeling that we had made a terrible mistake, that in our arrogance, we had set something in motion that we could never hope to control.

The air grew thick, charged with malevolent energy. Each breath was a struggle. Still, we pressed on, our voices rising in a desperate crescendo: to free Merlin, to save the world.

Or to damn it.

A blinding surge of energy erupted from the altar, slamming into us with the force of a tidal wave. I felt my feet leave the ground, my body careening through the air. The impact knocked the wind from my lungs as I crashed onto the cold stone floor.

"Michael?" I gasped, struggling to breathe. The air crackled with malevolence, heavy and oppressive.

A deep, guttural laugh echoed through the chamber, sending icy tendrils of fear crawling up my spine. This was no benevolent wizard's mirth; this was the sound of pure, unadulterated evil.

"What have we done?" I whispered, my voice trembling.

Michael's face was ashen as he met my gaze. "Jessica, I-"

His words were cut short as the shadows before us began to coalesce, twisting and writhing into a horrific form. Darkness and fire melded together, birthing a creature of nightmares.

The demon lord emerged, its eyes burning with an unholy light that seared into my very soul. I wanted to look away, to deny the reality of what stood before us, but I found myself paralyzed by its gaze.

"Ah, foolish mortals," it purred, its voice like gravel and silk. "How kind of you to provide me with such a grand entrance."

I felt the weight of my failure crushing down upon me. We had sought to free Merlin, to be the heroes of legend. Instead, we had unleashed something far worse.

"This wasn't supposed to happen," Michael muttered, his earlier confidence shattered.

The demon lord's laughter boomed once more, shaking the very foundations of the chamber. "And yet, here I am, thanks to your... misguided efforts."

I closed my eyes, willing it all to be a terrible dream. But when I opened them again, the nightmare remained. The world we had sought to save now lay at the feet of a conqueror, and we were the ones who had handed it to him on a silver platter.

I scrambled to my feet, my legs trembling beneath me. Michael's face mirrored the horror I felt, his skin ashen and eyes wide with disbelief. The air grew thick and heavy with malevolence that pressed against my chest, making each breath a struggle.

"Jessica," Michael whispered, his voice cracking, "what have we done?"

I couldn't answer. The demon lord's presence consumed everything; its power was a tangible force that threatened to crush us. My senses reeled, overwhelmed by the sheer wrongness of the creature before us.

A deep rumble shook the earth, and the world outside our chamber erupted into chaos. Through the ancient windows, I watched in horror as the sky turned an unnatural shade of crimson. Buildings in the distance began to crumble, their foundations giving way as if they were made of sand.

"Behold, the dawn of a new era," the demon lord's voice boomed, dripping with malicious glee. "Your world shall be remade in my image."

I turned to Michael, desperation clawing at my throat. "We need to stop this. There must be a way to"

My words were cut short as a deafening crack split the air. The ground beneath our feet lurched, sending us stumbling. Outside, trees toppled like dominoes, their roots torn from the earth.

"Stop it?" I laughed bitterly, the sound foreign even to my own ears. "We've unleashed hell itself. How do you propose we stop that?"

Michael's eyes darted around frantically, searching for an escape, a solution, anything. But I knew, deep in my bones, that we were far past the point of easy fixes. The world trembled and burned around us, a testament to our hubris and failure.

I stumbled through the ruins of what was once our sanctuary, my eyes stinging from the acrid smoke that filled the air. The others were scattered, lost in the chaos of our own making. I caught glimpses of familiar faces through the haze - Thalia's golden hair matted with blood, Marcus clutching his side as he limped forward.

"Regroup!" I shouted, my voice hoarse and barely audible over the cacophony of destruction. "We need to stick together!"

But even as the words left my lips, I felt the hollowness of my command. What were we now but broken fragments of a shattered dream?

My mind raced, each thought a sharp, accusatory blade. How could I have been so blind? So arrogant? The weight of my mistakes pressed down on me, threatening to crush my very soul.

"Jessica!" Michael's voice cut through the din. He appeared at my side, his face streaked with soot and despair. "We can't stay here. We need to-"

I cut him off, a bitter laugh escaping my lips. "Need to what, Michael? Run? Hide? We've doomed the world. There's nowhere left to go."

His hand reached for mine, a gesture once comforting, now a cruel reminder of all we'd lost. I pulled away, unable to bear his touch.

"This is my fault," I whispered, the words tasting like ash on my tongue. "I should have known better. I should have seen the signs."

Around us, the world continued to crumble, a symphony of destruction punctuated by screams and the crashing of stone. Yet all I could hear was the relentless echo of my own failures, and each regret a dagger twisting deeper into my heart.

Michael's fingers tightened around the ancient tome, his knuckles white with tension. I watched as he stared at its worn cover, his eyes haunted by the weight of our shared hubris.

"We were fools," he murmured, his voice barely audible above the cacophony of destruction. "Thinking we could control such power..."

I nodded, unable to find words to counter his despair. The air grew thick with smoke and the acrid stench of fear.

"We have to move," Kael's voice cut through our anguish, his usual wit replaced by grim determination. "The demon lord's destruction is spreading faster than we anticipated."

I turned to survey our surroundings, my heart sinking at the nightmarish landscape before us. Buildings crumbled like sandcastles, their foundations buckling under an unseen force. The sky, once blue, now roiled with angry crimson clouds.

"Where can we possibly go?" I asked, my voice hollow. "What haven't we already destroyed?"

Azhara's measured tones carried over the chaos. "We retreat to regroup, not to hide. Our path forward lies in facing our mistakes, not running from them."

As we stumbled through the ruins of our hubris, I couldn't help but wonder - had we truly freed Merlin or merely unleashed our own damnation?

A moment of eerie quiet descended upon us, the chaos momentarily muted as if the world itself held its breath. Thalia stepped forward, her silver hair catching the sickly light of the ruined sky. Her violet eyes, usually so full of mystery, now brimmed with an unfamiliar uncertainty.

"We are not lost," she began, her voice a whisper that seemed to carry on the wind. "The threads of fate, though tangled, still..."

I watched as her words trailed off, the weight of our predicament seeming to crush even her indomitable spirit. Thalia's gaze flickered to the horizon, where the demon lord's destruction painted the world in shades of ash and blood.

"What do you see, Thalia?" I asked, desperate for any shred of hope. "What future awaits us now?"

She turned to me, her face a mask of sorrow. "I see... darkness," she admitted, her usual poetic cadence faltering. "A void where once there were infinite possibilities."

Michael's hand found mine, his grip trembling. "We've doomed us all, haven't we?" he whispered.

I couldn't answer. The truth of our actions, the horror we'd unleashed, constricted my throat like a noose. We stood amidst the ruins of what was once a thriving city, now nothing more than a graveyard of broken dreams and shattered stone.

A deep, guttural laugh echoed through the air, seeming to come from everywhere and nowhere at once. It reverberated in my skull, a cruel reminder of the demon lord's victory - our failure.

"What have we done?" I breathed, the words tasting like ash on my tongue.

Michael's grip tightened. "We wanted to be heroes," he said, his voice hollow. "Instead, we've become the authors of the world's destruction."

As we stood there, surrounded by the consequences of our actions, I couldn't help but wonder - was this always our destiny? Or had we, in our arrogance, written our own tragic end?

CHAPTER 13

DARK NIGHT OF THE SOUL

The candlelight flickered, casting long shadows across the weathered pages of the ancient text before us. I could feel the weight of our failure pressing down, suffocating me with each labored breath. Michael sat across from me, his face a mask of anguish in the dim light.

"What have we done?" I whispered, my voice barely audible over the pounding of my heart. The words hung in the air, a confession of our shared sin.

Michael's eyes met mine, reflecting the horror I felt deep in my bones. We had unleashed something beyond our comprehension, something that now lurked in the shadows of our world.

I ran my trembling fingers over the arcane symbols etched into the yellowed parchment. Each curve and line seemed to pulse with malevolent energy, mocking our naivety. The room felt smaller, the walls closing in as the magnitude of our actions settled upon us.

"The demons," I continued, my voice cracking. "We've set them free. All those people..." I couldn't finish the thought, the faces of the innocent flashing before my eyes.

Michael reached across the table, his hand finding mine. His touch was cold, a stark reminder of the chill that had settled into our souls. We sat in silence, the gravity of our mistake pressing down upon us like a physical weight.

I closed my eyes, trying to shut out the horrors we had witnessed, but they played on repeat in my mind. The screams, the chaos, the destruction - all because of our hubris. We had sought power beyond our understanding, and now the world would pay the price.

"Jessica," Michael's voice was low and strained. "We need to fix this."

I nodded, but doubt gnawed at me. How could we possibly undo what we had done? The demons were loose, wreaking havoc across the land. We were just two people, in over our heads and drowning in guilt.

The candle sputtered, threatening to plunge us into darkness. I stared at the flame, wondering if this was how hope died - not with a bang, but with a quiet flicker.

Michael's face contorted, a mixture of anguish and fury etching deep lines into his weary features. His eyes, once bright with the thrill of discovery, now smoldered with barely contained rage.

"Fix this?" he spat, his voice dripping with bitterness. "How can we possibly hope to rectify such a catastrophic mistake? We've unleashed hell itself, Jessica. We're not heroes; we're harbingers of doom."

His words cut deep, echoing my own doubts. I flinched, feeling the weight of his accusation. But wasn't it justified? We had meddled with forces beyond our comprehension, drunk on the promise of power and knowledge.

"Perhaps," I whispered, my voice trembling, "perhaps Thalia could guide us. She might know a way to—"

"Thalia?" Michael interrupted, his laugh hollow and mirthless. "What makes you think she'd help us now? We ignored her warnings, and look where it's gotten us."

I fell silent, my mind a maelstrom of conflicting emotions.

Part of me longed to flee, to abandon this ill-fated quest and lose myself in obscurity. Yet a small, persistent voice whispered of hope and redemption.

"We can't just give up," I murmured, more to myself than to Michael.

He sighed, the anger draining from him, leaving only exhaustion in its wake. "Can't we? Wouldn't the world be better off without our interference?"

I had no answer. The silence stretched between us, filled with unspoken fears and regrets. Our past sins loomed large, threatening to consume us entirely.

I couldn't bear it any longer. The suffocating weight of our failure pressed down on me, threatening to crush what little resolve I had left. With a sudden, jerky movement, I stood, my chair scraping harshly against the floor. The sound echoed in the oppressive silence, a discordant note in our symphony of despair.

I stumbled to the window, seeking... what? Escape? Absolution? My reflection stared back at me, a ghostly apparition superimposed over the darkened sky. Those haunted eyes, once alight with determination, now seemed hollow and lost. Was this truly what I'd become?

"Jessica," Michael's voice drifted to me, a weary whisper. "What do you see out there?"

I pressed my forehead against the cool glass. "Nothing," I replied, my breath fogging the pane. "Just darkness. Endless darkness."

Behind me, I heard Michael's fists slam against the table. "Damnit!" he hissed. "We should never have started this. We're not... we're not strong enough for this."

I turned, watching him. His lanky frame was hunched over the table, and hands clenched so tightly his knuckles had gone white. The eager curiosity that once animated his features had been replaced by a mask of anguish. My heart ached at the sight.

"Maybe you're right," I admitted the words tasting like ash in my mouth. "Maybe we should just... give up."

Michael's head snapped up, his eyes meeting mine. For a moment, I saw a flicker of the old Michael – determined, hopeful. But it was snuffed out almost immediately, replaced by a storm of doubt.

"Could we?" he asked, his voice small. "Just... walk away from it all?"

I closed my eyes, picturing the carnage we'd unleashed. The screams of the innocent echoed in my mind, a hellish cacophony that I knew would haunt me for the rest of my days. "No," I whispered. "I don't think we can."

The silence that followed was deafening, a weight that pressed down on us both. The room seemed to shrink, the shadows in the corners creeping closer as if they sought to devour us. I could feel the walls closing in, trapping us with our guilt and despair.

My breath caught in my throat as I turned back to Michael. I could barely see him through the tears that blurred my vision. "Michael," I choked out, my voice trembling, "do you really think we can do this? Summon the dragons?"

I bit my lip, tasting blood. The metallic flavor reminded me of the carnage we'd witnessed, the lives we'd destroyed. My hand unconsciously moved to the pen in my pocket, fingers itching to chew on it, to give my anxiety an outlet.

"I'm terrified," I confessed, the words spilling out like a poisonous flood. "What if we're not strong enough? What if we fail again?"

Michael's eyes met mine, and I saw my own fear reflected there. He opened his mouth to speak, but no words came out. At that moment, I realized that he was just as lost as I was, just as haunted by the weight of our actions.

The enormity of our task loomed before us, a mountain of impossibility that threatened to crush us beneath its weight. And yet, beneath the terror and doubt, a small spark of determination still flickered. It was faint, barely alive, but it was there.

I took a shaky breath, waiting for Michael's response, silently pleading for him to give me something, anything, to cling to in this ocean of despair.

Michael rose, his chair scraping against the floor like nails on a chalkboard. I winced as he crossed the room, his footsteps echoing in the oppressive silence. When his hand touched my shoulder, I nearly flinched. It was meant to comfort, I knew, but the weight of it felt like an anchor, dragging me deeper into the abyss of our shared guilt.

"We've unleashed hell," I whispered, my voice barely audible. "All those people..."

"I know," Michael murmured, his fingers tightening on my shoulder. "God, Jessica, I know."

I turned to face him, searching his eyes for any sign of hope. But all I saw was a reflection of my own torment, a mirror of the darkness that had taken root in our souls.

"The streets run red with blood we spilled," I said, the words tasting like ash on my tongue. "And for what? Our arrogance? Our foolish belief that we could control forces beyond our comprehension?"

Michael's jaw clenched, a muscle twitching beneath his skin. "We thought we were doing the right thing," he said, but the words rang hollow.

I laughed, a bitter, broken sound. "And look where that's gotten us. Look at the chaos we've unleashed."

As we stood there, the weight of our actions pressing down on us like a physical force, I couldn't help but wonder if this guilt would be the thing that finally tore us apart. We were bound by our sins, yes, but could we bear the burden together? Or would it ultimately destroy us both?

The silence stretched between us, a yawning chasm filled with unspoken doubts and festering regrets. I could feel the weight of our decision looming over us, an invisible sword of Damocles ready to fall. The choice before us was stark and merciless: press on with our doomed quest or surrender to the crushing despair that threatened to consume us both.

I gazed out the window, my reflection a ghostly apparition against the inky darkness beyond. The night seemed to whisper of our transgressions, a soft, insidious voice that wormed its way into my mind. How easy it would be to give in, to let the darkness claim us...

But then, unbidden, an image of Thalia Moonshadow flickered in my mind's eye. Her enigmatic smile, those violet eyes that seemed to hold the secrets of the universe... A faint glimmer of hope stirred in my chest, fragile as a butterfly's wing.

I drew in a shaky breath, tasting the acrid tang of fear on my tongue. "Michael," I said, my voice barely above a whisper, "what if... what if we sought out Thalia again?"

He turned to me, his brow furrowed. "Thalia? The seer?"

I nodded, the words tumbling out in a desperate rush. "She might be able to guide us, to show us a way forward. I know it's a long shot, but..." I trailed off, suddenly uncertain.

Michael's eyes searched mine, a storm of emotions playing across his face. "Do you really think she can help us? After everything we've done?"

I swallowed hard, fighting back the wave of guilt that threatened to drown me. "I don't know. But it's better than giving up, isn't it? Better than letting the darkness win?"

Michael's jaw clenched, the muscles working beneath his weathered skin. For a moment, I feared he'd refuse, that the weight of our sins had finally crushed his indomitable spirit. But then he nodded, his eyes gleaming with a mixture of resignation and determination that made my heart ache.

"You're right," he said, his voice low and rough. "We can't abandon our mission now. Not after... everything."

The unspoken words hung between us, heavy as lead. Not after the lives lost, the chaos unleashed. Not after we'd torn the very fabric of reality asunder with our hubris.

I reached out, my fingers brushing his arm. "Together, then?"

He covered my hand with his own, calloused and warm. "Together."

We moved as one, our footsteps echoing in the oppressive silence as we made our way to the door. Each step felt like a battle, as if the very air resisted our passage, clinging to us with spectral fingers.

As we crossed the threshold, I cast one last glance at the ancient text lying open on the table. Its pages seemed to flutter in a nonexistent breeze, and for a moment, I could have sworn I heard the faintest whisper of draconic voices.

I shuddered, turning away. Our path was uncertain, fraught with dangers I could scarcely imagine. But as we moved forward, side by side, I felt a flicker of something I'd thought long extinguished.

Hope: fragile and fleeting, but they are all the same.

I clung to that feeble spark of hope as we descended the winding staircase, each step creaking beneath our feet like the groans of tortured souls. The air grew thick and oppressive as if the very walls were closing in around us.

"Do you think..." I began, my voice barely above a whisper, "Do you think we'll ever truly make amends?"

Michael's reply came slowly, measured. "I don't know, Jess, but we have to try."

His words echoed in the hollow chambers of my mind, a painful reminder of our shared burden. I could still see the faces of those we'd failed, their accusatory stares haunting my every waking moment.

We emerged into the courtyard, the night sky a vast, starless void above us. The darkness seemed to pulse, alive with malevolent energy. I shivered, drawing closer to Michael.

"It feels like we're walking into the maw of some great beast," I murmured, unable to shake the dread that clung to me like a second skin.

Michael's hand found mine, a lifeline in the encroaching gloom. "Perhaps we are," he said softly. "But remember, even in the darkest depths, there's always a way out. We just have to find it."

I nodded, swallowing hard against the lump in my throat. As we set out into the night, I couldn't help but feel we were marching toward our doom. Yet that tiny ember of hope still flickered within me, fragile but unyielding.

Our journey continued, fraught with uncertainty. But we moved forward together into whatever darkness awaited us.

CHAPTER 14

RESURRECTION

I stared into the flickering shadows, my soul as hollow as this forsaken chamber. Beside me, Michael's face was a mask of anguish, mirroring the despair that gnawed at my insides. We were lost, adrift in a sea of hopelessness.

Then she appeared.

Thalia Moonshadow glided before us, her silver hair shimmering like starlight. Her mere presence seemed to push back the encroaching darkness. I wanted to cling to that light, but shame kept me rooted in shadow.

"Jessica. Michael." Her voice was soft as silk, yet it cut through my spiraling thoughts. "The dragons await. Their realm trembles on the edge of our reality, yearning to be awakened."

I laughed bitterly. "And we're supposed to be the ones to do it? We're broken, Thalia. How can we possibly—"

"Hush, child." Her violet eyes seemed to pierce my very soul. "The power to reshape worlds lies dormant within you. It always has."

Michael stirred beside me. "But the cost... What we've done to get here..."

Memories of blood and betrayal flashed through my mind.

The weight of our sins pressed down, threatening to crush what little resolve remained.

Thalia's voice took on a lyrical quality, weaving through the air like smoke. "The past is etched in stone, but the future is clay in your hands. Remember why you began this journey. The dragons' return will herald a new age, one of balance and redemption."

Her words stirred something within me, a faint ember of hope I thought long extinguished. Yet doubt still gnawed. "And if we fail?"

"Then all fall to darkness," Thalia said simply. "But I have seen glimpses of what may be. The path is treacherous but not impassable."

I closed my eyes, feeling the weight of destiny settle upon my shoulders. When I opened them again, Thalia's gaze held mine, an anchor in the storm of my thoughts.

"Are you ready to embrace your calling?" she asked, her voice a rhythmic cadence that seemed to resonate with the very fabric of reality.

I glanced at Michael, seeing a flicker of determination in his eyes that mirrored my own growing resolve. The chamber suddenly felt charged with possibility, the air thick with the promise of cosmic change.

"We are," I whispered, the words tasting of both fear and hope on my tongue.

As Thalia's final words faded, Michael and I exchanged a glance. In his eyes, I saw a reflection of my own trepidation but also a spark of renewed purpose. We nodded, a silent pact forged in the depths of our shared desperation.

"The components," I murmured, my voice hoarse, "we must gather them."

Michael rose, his movements stiff as if shaking off a great weight. "The Starfire crystal?"

I nodded, crossing the chamber to an ornate chest. My fingers trembled as I lifted the lid, revealing the pulsing gem within. Its light seemed to pierce the gloom, casting eerie shadows that danced along the walls like specters of our past failures.

"Do you truly believe we can undo what we've done?" Michael asked, his voice barely above a whisper.

I clutched the crystal, its warmth seeping into my palm. "I don't know," I admitted. "But what choice do we have? The weight of our sins... it's unbearable."

As we moved about the chamber, collecting herbs, ancient texts, and arcane symbols, each item felt heavy with significance. Every deliberate action was a step toward either our salvation or our final damnation.

"The dragon's scale," Michael said, holding up the iridescent object. "It almost seems alive."

I shuddered, remembering the terrible price paid for that scale. "Let's hope it's enough to bridge the gap between our realm and theirs."

As we prepared, Thalia's presence lingered like a comforting shadow. Yet even her serene demeanor couldn't fully quell the storm of doubt raging within me. What terrors would we unleash in our quest for redemption?

The ritual space loomed before us, a perfect circle etched into the cold stone floor. Flickering candles surrounded it, their flames casting long, sinister shadows that seemed to reach for us with grasping fingers. The air hung heavy, thick with the scent of incense and the metallic tang of fear.

"It's time," I whispered, my voice sounding foreign to my own ears.

Michael nodded, his face a mask of determination belied by the tremor in his hands. "Jessica, I... what if we fail?"

I met his gaze, seeing my own doubts reflected in his eyes. "Then we'll have earned our damnation twice over."

We stepped into the circle, our hearts thundering in unison. The boundary tingled against my skin, a reminder of the power we were about to unleash. I clutched the Starfire crystal, its pulsing light seeming to sync with my racing pulse.

"Remember the words," I cautioned, my throat tight. "One mistake and-"

"I know," Michael interrupted, his voice stronger than I expected. "We've come too far to falter now."

As we began to chant, our voices merged into a haunting melody that echoed through the chamber. The words felt like poison on my tongue, each syllable a reminder of the dark path that led us here. Yet, as our voices rose and fell in eerie harmony, I felt a spark of hope ignite within the depths of my despair.

"Voca dracones antiques," we intoned, the words vibrating through my very bones. "Porta aperire inter mundos."

The candles flickered wildly, and for a moment, I thought I glimpsed shapes forming in the shadows – accusatory faces of those we'd wronged. I pushed the vision aside, focusing on the task at hand. Our redemption – or our doom – lay on the other side of this ritual.

The air around us crackled with energy, a tangible force that pulsed with each word spoken. I could feel it coiling around us, seeping into our very souls. The candles' flames danced erratically, casting grotesque shadows that writhed on the walls like tortured spirits.

"Is this... is this right?" Michael whispered, his voice barely audible over our chanting.

I hesitated, doubt gnawing at my resolve. "I don't know," I admitted, my words nearly lost in the swirling chaos. "But we can't stop now."

Our eyes met, and I saw my own fear reflected in Michael's gaze. For a moment, I was back in that cursed village, the screams of the innocent ringing in my ears. We'd done unspeakable things to get here, and now...

"Focus," Thalia's calm voice cut through my spiraling thoughts. She stood just outside the circle, her presence an anchor in the tempest of our guilt and fear. "Remember why you're here."

I gritted my teeth, forcing the words out. "For redemption," I muttered, more to myself than to anyone else.

Michael nodded, his jaw set. "For a chance to make things right."

We pressed on, our voices growing stronger. The energy in the room intensified, and I could feel something vast and ancient stirring beyond the veil of reality. My heart raced, equal parts terror and exhilaration.

"We're close," I gasped between verses. "I can feel it."

Michael's hand found mine, squeezing tightly. "Together," he said, his eyes blazing with determination. "Whatever comes next."

I squeezed back, drawing strength from his touch and Thalia's unwavering gaze. The shadows danced, the air crackled, and we chanted on, teetering on the precipice of either salvation or damnation.

The chamber plunged into an inky darkness, swallowing even the feeble light of our guttering candles. My voice faltered, a chill creeping up my spine. "Michael?" I whispered, suddenly unsure if he was still beside me.

His grip on my hand tightened. "I'm here, Jessica. Keep going."

We pressed on, our words echoing in the void. A low rumble began to build, vibrating through the stone beneath our feet. It grew, a primal force that set my teeth on edge and made my bones ache.

"The dragons," I breathed in . Awe and terror are warring within me. "They're coming."

Michael's voice shook slightly as he replied, "Let's hope we haven't damned ourselves further by summoning them."

The rumbling crescendoed, and I feared the very chamber might collapse around us. Just as I thought I could bear no more, reality itself seemed to tear.

A vortex erupted before us, a maelstrom of light and shadow that hurt to look upon. It pulsed with otherworldly energy, each throb sending waves of power washing over us. The air filled with a deafening roar, ancient and terrible.

"By all the gods," Michael gasped. "What have we done?"

I couldn't answer. My mind reeled, overwhelmed by the sheer magnitude of what we'd unleashed. As I stared into the swirling chaos, I caught glimpses of another realm – vast and beautiful and utterly alien.

"The Ethereal Realm," I whispered, remembering Thalia's teachings. "We've opened the way."

From the heart of that swirling vortex, a massive form began to emerge. At first, I could only make out a silhouette, colossal and serpentine. But as it pushed through the boundary between worlds, details snapped into focus with terrifying clarity.

Scales like living starlight rippled across its body, each one a galaxy unto itself. Its eyes blazed with an inner fire that seemed to pierce my very soul. I felt stripped bare, all my sins and doubts laid naked before that ancient gaze.

"Michael," I choked out, my voice barely a whisper. "Do you see it?"

He didn't respond, and for a moment, I feared he'd fled. But then I felt his hand grasp mine, trembling but present.

"I see it," he murmured. "God help me, I see it."

The dragon – for what else could it be? – fully emerged, its wings unfurling to span the entirety of the chamber. It was beautiful and terrible, a being of pure, primal power that defied mortal comprehension.

And it wasn't alone.

Behind it, more shapes began to push through the portal: dragons of every hue and form, each one a testament to magic beyond our wildest imaginings. They poured forth in an endless stream, filling the air with the beat of wings and the crackle of elemental energy.

I should have been terrified. Perhaps a part of me was. But as I stood there, transfixed by the majesty before me, I felt something else stirring in my chest – a fierce, wild hope.

"We did it," I breathed, squeezing Michael's hand. "We actually did it."

The largest dragon, its scales shimmering like starlight,

lowered its massive head until its eye was level with mine. At that moment, I felt the weight of eons pressing down upon me. The dragon's gaze held ancient wisdom, unfathomable power, and... recognition.

I couldn't breathe. I couldn't think. The world narrowed to that single point of contact between our eyes.

We see you, Jessica of the mortal realm, a voice thundered in my mind. *We see your struggles, your doubts, your unwavering resolve.*

My knees nearly buckled. "Michael," I gasped, "can you hear-"

"Yes," he whispered, his voice thick with emotion. "I hear them, too."

The dragon's attention shifted to Michael, and I felt him stiffen beside me. "Your path has been long and treacherous, Michael the Steadfast. Yet you have not faltered."

A pact, unspoken but binding, seemed to form in that charged moment. We were no longer mere mortals fumbling in the dark; we were chosen, entrusted with a power and purpose beyond our comprehension.

The last dragon, a creature of midnight blue and silver, slipped through the portal. As its tail cleared the threshold, the swirling vortex collapsed with a deafening boom that shook the very foundations of the chamber.

Silence fell, heavy and absolute.

I turned to Michael, seeing my own awe and trepidation mirrored in his eyes. "What have we done?" I whispered, the enormity of our success crashing over me like a tidal wave.

He shook his head slowly, a wry smile tugging at his lips. "Opened Pandora's box, I fear. But perhaps... perhaps this time, hope isn't left trapped inside."

A soft rustle of fabric drew my attention. Thalia stepped forward, her silver hair shimmering in the dim light like a river of moonbeams. Her enigmatic smile sent a shiver down my spine - was it reassurance or a portent of trials to come?

"You've done well," she murmured, her violet eyes seeming to peer into the very depths of my soul. "But this is merely the beginning."

I swallowed hard, and my throat suddenly dried. "The beginning of what, exactly?"

Thalia's gaze swept over us, her expression inscrutable. "Of a journey that will reshape the very fabric of our world."

Michael shifted beside me, his shoulder brushing mine. The brief contact steadied me, grounding me in the moment. "And what role do we play in this... reshaping?" he asked, his voice tight with barely contained apprehension.

A haunting melody seemed to weave through Thalia's words as she responded, "You are the catalysts, the bridge between worlds. The dragons have acknowledged you and bound their fates to yours."

My mind reeled. Catalysts? Bound fates? The weight of responsibility settled over me like a shroud, threatening to suffocate. I closed my eyes, willing the room to stop spinning.

"But we're just... us," I whispered, more to myself than to anyone else. "How can we possibly-"

"You are more than you know," Thalia interrupted, her tone gentle but firm. "The battles ahead will test you, break you, and forge you anew. But remember this moment when the dragons looked upon you and saw worth."

I opened my eyes, meeting Thalia's gaze. In her violet depths, I saw reflected the vastness of the Ethereal Realm, the cosmic dance of stars and galaxies. For a heartbeat, I understood the true scope of what we'd set in motion.

"We're not ready," I breathed, terror and exhilaration warring within me.

Thalia's smile deepened, a mystery wrapped in an enigma. "No one ever is, dear one. But ready or not, destiny awaits."

CHAPTER 15

BATTLE OR SHOWDOWN

The sky split open with a deafening crack, and they descended.

Dragons. Magnificent and terrible, their scales gleamed like polished armor even in the gloom. Their wings blotted out what little light remained as storm clouds roiled above. Thunder or roars? I could no longer distinguish.

My breath caught in my throat. Beside me, Jessica trembled, her eyes wide with a mixture of awe and terror. "Michael," she whispered, her voice barely audible above the cacophony, "what have we done?"

I couldn't answer. My mind reeled, struggling to comprehend the enormity of what we were witnessing. The ancient parchment had warned us, but we hadn't truly believed it. How foolish we'd been.

As the dragons spiraled lower, their massive forms becoming clearer, I felt a curious shift in the air. The witches and warlocks around us, our supposed allies in this madness, straightened their backs and lifted their chins. Their fear was palpable, but so was their determination.

"Stand fast!" someone shouted, the words carried on the wind.

I glanced at Jessica and saw the resolve hardening in her eyes.

"We can't undo this," I said, my voice sounding hollow to my own ears. "But perhaps we can still make it right."

She nodded, her fingers intertwining with mine. The gesture should have been comforting, but I felt only the chill of dread. What price would we pay for our hubris?

The dragons landed, the earth trembling beneath their weight. At that moment, as their eyes – ancient and knowing – swept over us, I realized the true depth of our folly. We had unleashed something beyond our comprehension, and now we stood on the precipice of a battle that would shape the fate of worlds.

My heart raced; each beat a reminder of my mortality in the face of these cosmic beings. Yet, as I looked around at the gathered witches and warlocks, their faces etched with a mixture of fear and fierce determination, I felt a flicker of hope.

Perhaps, just perhaps, we might survive this after all. But at what cost? The thought gnawed at me, a worm of doubt burrowing deep into my soul.

The ground shook as Azhara Stormscale landed, her emerald scales casting an eerie glow in the dim light. My breath caught in my throat as she towered over us, her presence both terrifying and awe-inspiring. I couldn't help but wonder if we were mere insects to her, insignificant specks in the grand tapestry of existence.

"Children of magic," Azhara's voice resonated, each word heavy with ancient power. "The hour of reckoning is upon us."

I shivered, her words seeming to penetrate my very being. Was this how it felt to stand before a god?

"We stand at the precipice of oblivion," she continued, her eyes sweeping over our ranks. "But it is in the darkest of times that our light must shine brightest."

A murmur rippled through the crowd. I heard hope in those whispers but also fear. How many of us would fall before this day was done?

"Remember," I whispered to myself, "we chose this path." But had we truly understood the consequences?

Azhara's speech continued each word kindling a fire within us. Yet even as courage bloomed, a chill ran down my spine. For beyond her majestic form, I saw them – the demonic hordes.

They emerged from the shadows like a nightmare given flesh. Their grotesque forms a mockery of life. The air grew thick with the stench of sulfur and decay.

"Steady," Jessica hissed beside me, her fingers tightening on her staff. "We knew this was coming."

But knowing and seeing were two very different things. As the demons surged forward, their hunger for destruction palpable, I felt my resolve waver.

"Stand ready!" Azhara's voice boomed, cutting through my rising panic.

I raised my hands, dark energy crackling at my fingertips. This was it – the moment that would define us all. As the horde rushed toward us, I couldn't help but wonder: in our quest to save the world, had we damned it instead?

The sky erupted in chaos. Dragons swooped overhead, their massive forms casting fleeting shadows across the battlefield. A torrent of fire cascaded from their jaws, scorching the earth and turning the air to ash.

"Now!" I heard Azhara's command ring out.

My hands moved of their own accord, weaving intricate patterns in the air. Beside me, Jessica's voice rose in a haunting chant. Our magic intertwined, creating a shimmering barrier before us.

But would it be enough?

The demons crashed against our defenses like a tidal wave of nightmares. I felt each impact reverberate through my bones, threatening to shatter my concentration.

"Hold the line!" someone shouted. Was it me? I couldn't be sure anymore.

Through the haze of smoke and magic, I caught glimpses of Azhara. She moved like liquid grace, and her emerald scales a blur as she tore through the demonic ranks. Her presence ignited a spark of hope within me, but it was quickly smothered by doubt.

"We can't keep this up forever," I muttered, my voice hoarse from the acrid air.

Jessica's eyes met mine, reflecting the same fear I felt. "We don't have to," she replied grimly. "We just have to last long enough."

Long enough for what? I wanted to ask, but the words died on my lips as another wave of demons surged forward. Our barrier flickered, and for a moment, I thought this might be the end.

Then Azhara's voice cut through the din: "Stand fast, my friends! Our strength lies not in our power but in our unity!"

I clung to those words like a lifeline, even as the darkness pressed in around us. But a nagging voice in the back of my mind whispered, what if our unity isn't enough? What if we've already lost?

The tide of battle shifted again, a momentary reprieve as our spells found their mark. Demons shrieked and writhed, their twisted forms crumbling to ash. But my triumph was fleeting, a bitter taste on my tongue.

"Michael," Jessica called, her voice strained. "I can't... I can't hold it much longer."

I turned to her and saw the trembling in her hands as she wove another protection charm. The sight of her, so strong yet so fragile, tore at my heart. I reached out, clasping her fingers in mine.

"Just a little longer," I whispered, though I had no right to ask it of her. Of any of them.

The sky above us roiled with unnatural storm clouds, a mirror to the chaos below. Lightning crackled, illuminating the endless sea of demons still pouring forth. How many had we felt? How many more would come?

"There's no end to them," a nearby warlock moaned, his face a mask of despair.

I wanted to offer words of comfort, but what could I say? The truth was, I shared his fear. With each spell I cast, each demon I banished, the weight of our task pressed heavier upon me. We were but mortals, playing at godhood in a game we couldn't hope to win.

And yet, we fought on. What choice did we have? The alternatives were too terrible to contemplate.

"Jessica," I murmured, my voice barely audible above the din. "Do you remember why we started this?"

She met my gaze, her eyes glistening with unshed tears. "To save the world," she replied, a ghost of a smile on her lips.

I nodded, swallowing hard. "To save the world," I echoed, though the words rang hollow in my ears. Had we damned it instead?

A deafening roar shook the battlefield, and I watched in horror as our eastern flank crumbled. Witches and warlocks fell, their screams lost in the cacophony of battle. The acrid stench of brimstone and charred flesh assaulted my nostrils, nearly bringing me to my knees.

"We can't hold," I choked out, my throat raw from shouting spells. "We're going to—"

But my words were cut short by a voice that seemed to come from everywhere and nowhere at once. Azhara Stormscale, her emerald scales glinting even in the dim light, had taken to the sky.

"Stand fast!" she thundered, her words resonating in my very bones. "We are the last line of defense between these abominations and everything we hold dear!"

I wanted to believe her. Oh, how I longed to. But the doubt that had taken root in my heart whispered insidiously, reminding me of all we'd already lost.

"What if we've already failed?" I murmured more to myself than to anyone else.

Azhara's piercing gaze found mine, and for a moment, I felt stripped bare, all my fears and insecurities laid out before her.

"Every breath you take is an act of defiance," she declared. "Every spell you cast pushes back the darkness. We fight not because victory is certain but because the alternative is unthinkable."

Her words stirred something within me—a flicker of hope I thought long extinguished. I raised my staff, drawing upon reserves of power I didn't know I possessed.

"For everything we've lost," I shouted, my voice cracking. "And everything we've yet to save!"

As one, we surged forward, our magic a brilliant tapestry woven against the encroaching darkness. But even as I fought, a part of me wondered: how long could we keep this up? And at what cost?

I cast a desperate glance skyward, my heart pounding in my chest. The dragons, those majestic beings of legend, circled above us like vengeful gods. Their scales glimmered with an other-worldly light, a stark contrast to the hellish landscape below.

"Now!" Azhara's voice rang out, a clarion call that cut through the cacophony of battle.

As if orchestrated by some cosmic conductor, the dragons dove in perfect unison. Their jaws gaped wide, revealing infernos barely contained within. I watched, transfixed, as they unleashed their fury upon the demonic horde.

The world erupted in fire and chaos.

"Jessica!" Michael's voice snapped me back to reality. He stood beside me, his face smeared with ash and blood. "We need to regroup. This is our chance!"

I nodded, my throat too tight for words. As we retreated, the scorched earth crunched beneath our feet. The acrid stench of burnt flesh assaulted my nostrils, and I fought the urge to retch.

"How many?" I whispered, dreading the answer.

Michael's eyes, usually so warm and reassuring, were haunted. "Too many," he replied, his voice barely audible over the din of battle.

We crested a small rise, and the full extent of our losses became apparent. Bodies littered the ground – friend and foe alike. Some still twitched, clinging desperately to life. Others lay eerily still, their vacant eyes staring accusingly at the uncaring sky.

"Oh gods," I choked out, my knees threatening to buckle. "What have we done?"

Michael's hand found mine, squeezing gently. "What we had to," he said, but I could hear the doubt in his voice.

I closed my eyes, willing the horrific scene away. But it was burned into my memory, a stark reminder of the price of our resistance. When I opened them again, I saw the same anguish reflected in the faces of our surviving allies.

"Was it worth it?" I asked, the words escaping before I could stop them.

Michael didn't answer immediately. When he did, his voice was heavy with the weight of command. "It has to be," he said. "Otherwise, their sacrifice means nothing."

I nodded, swallowing hard against the lump in my throat. As we prepared for the next assault, I couldn't shake the feeling that we were merely delaying the inevitable. How much more could we endure before we broke completely?

The stench of death clung to us like a shroud as we regrouped, our ragged band of survivors huddling close. I caught Vesper's eye, their shadowy form flickering at the edges of my vision. For a moment, I thought I glimpsed something akin to concern in those fathomless eyes.

"The veil grows thin," Vesper whispered, their ethereal voice sending shivers down my spine. "Can you feel it, little one? The boundaries blur."

I nodded, unable to find my voice. The air felt heavy, charged with an otherworldly energy that set my teeth on edge.

"We stand together," Michael declared, his voice carrying across our battered lines. "Or we fall as one."

A murmur of agreement rippled through the ranks. I felt it then – a spark of something. Hope? Determination? Whatever it was, it kindled a fire in my chest.

"The shadows whisper of unity," Vesper mused, their form

shifting like smoke. "Perhaps there is power in such... mortal concepts."

As if in response to our renewed resolve, a bone-chilling howl echoed across the battlefield. The demons were regrouping, their malevolent presence casting an unnatural darkness over the land.

"They come," I breathed, my hand tightening on my weapon. "Gods help us all."

Michael's jaw clenched. "The gods are silent. We must help ourselves."

I couldn't shake the feeling that we were staring into the abyss. And the abyss, hungry and merciless, was staring back.

The air grew thick and cloying as if the very atmosphere sought to choke us. I swallowed hard, tasting ash and despair on my tongue. My gaze swept across our ragged line of defenders, their faces etched with exhaustion and grim determination.

"Azhara," I called my voice barely a rasp. "What do you see?"

The dragon-turned-warrior stood motionless, her emerald eyes fixed on the writhing darkness beyond. When she spoke, her words carried the weight of prophecy.

"The end," she murmured, "or perhaps... a beginning."

A chill raced down my spine. I wanted to ask more, to demand answers, but the words died in my throat as the first wave of demons crested the horizon.

"Hold fast!" Michael's voice rang out, steady despite the tremor I saw in his hands. "Remember why we fight!"

Kael appeared at my side, his usual mischievous grin replaced by a mask of grim focus. "Well, this is cheery," he quipped, but the levity fell flat. "Any last words of wisdom?"

I choked back a bitter laugh. "Don't die?"

"Solid advice," he nodded, his eyes never leaving the approaching horde.

As the demons drew near, their howls rising to a deafening crescendo, I felt a curious calm settle over me. Was this acceptance? Or had fear finally pushed me beyond its reach?

"Whatever comes," Lyra's voice cut through the chaos, her silver hair a beacon in the gloom, "we face it together."

The words hung in the air, a fragile promise. As the first demon breached our lines, I couldn't shake the feeling that this moment – this terrible, pivotal instant – would echo through eternity.

We charged forward, our fates intertwined, our souls laid bare before the coming storm.

CHAPTER 16

CLIMAX

The sky bled crimson as chaos erupted around us. Dragons' roars shook the very air, their massive forms writhing against a sea of writhing darkness. Demonic shrieks pierced my ears as foul creatures clawed and gnashed, thirsting for our destruction. Spells crackled and fizzed, streaking across the battlefield in dazzling arcs.

I gripped my staff tighter, knuckles white. "Jessica, watch your flank!" I called out, my voice hoarse.

She whirled, eyes wide with fear, and blasted back an approaching demon with a burst of arcane energy. "Thanks," she panted. "Michael, I don't know how much longer we can hold them off."

My heart raced, dread coiling in my gut. We were vastly outnumbered, our magic depleting with each passing moment. The demons pressed in, a writhing mass of claws and fangs.

"We have to keep fighting," I growled, more to convince myself than her. "We can't let them break through."

But could we truly stem this infernal tide? Doubt gnawed at me, memories of our foolish actions that led to this catastrophe. The ancient parchment, the forbidden incantation... what fools we'd been.

A demon lunged for Jessica. I reacted on instinct, hurling a fireball that reduced it to ash. She flashed me a grateful smile, but exhaustion was etched in every line of her face.

"Michael," she whispered, "what have we done?"

The question hung between us, heavy with unspoken guilt. I had no answer, only the burning determination to survive this nightmare of our own making.

"We'll find a way," I lied, my voice steady despite the tremor in my hands. "We always do."

But as another wave of demons surged forward, their unholy shrieks filling the air, I wondered if, this time, our luck had finally run out.

A deafening roar shattered the sky, drowning out even the demonic cacophony. I looked up, my heart leaping with a desperate hope I dared not trust.

Azhara Stormscale, resplendent in her emerald glory, burst through the roiling clouds. Her scales glittered like a thousand precious gems, each movement a fluid dance of power and grace. Behind her, a legion of dragons unfurled their wings, their eyes blazing with ancient fury.

"The Emerald Sentinel," Jessica breathed, her voice tinged with awe and relief.

I couldn't tear my gaze away as Azhara opened her maw, unleashing a torrent of lightning that split the demon ranks. The air crackled with ozone and the scent of otherworldly power.

"Perhaps we're not doomed after all," I muttered, a sardonic smile twisting my lips. But even as I watched the dragons rain destruction upon our foes, a nagging voice whispered that we didn't deserve salvation. Not after what we'd done.

Azhara's voice, melodious yet thunderous, echoed across the battlefield. "Stand fast, mortals! We shall not let the balance fall!"

For a moment, hope surged. But then, a chilling laugh rose from the depths of the demon horde. A figure, cloaked in shadows that seemed to devour light itself, emerged.

"Ah, little dragons," it hissed, its voice like nails on slate. "How kind of you to join our feast."

The demon lord raised its hands, and a wave of darkness swept across the field. Dragons faltered mid-flight, their fire sputtering. Jessica stumbled beside me, her magic flickering like a candle in the wind.

"Michael," she gasped, "I can't... I can't feel my power."

I reached for my own magic and found only emptiness. Cold dread settled in my stomach as the demon lord's laughter echoed once more.

"Did you truly think you could stand against us?" it mocked. "Your hubris will be your undoing."

As the demons closed in, their eyes gleaming with unholy hunger, I couldn't help but think it was right. We had brought this upon ourselves, and now... now we would pay the price.

I gripped my useless sword, knuckles white, as the demons advanced. The acrid stench of brimstone choked the air. Then, without warning, a blinding light split the sky.

It was as if a star had descended, searing away the darkness. The light pulsed, growing stronger, and from its center emerged a figure I'd only heard of in whispered legends.

Merlin.

His presence hit like a physical force, driving demons and humans alike to their knees. I squinted against the radiance, my heart pounding. Was this salvation? Or is it merely another cruel twist of fate?

"The Warlock comes," Jessica breathed beside me, her voice tinged with awe and... fear?

I understood her trepidation. We'd committed unspeakable acts to survive. What judgment would Merlin pass on us?

The demon lord's earlier bravado evaporated. It shrieked, "Impossible! You were banished!"

Merlin's voice rumbled like distant thunder. "Did you think the cosmos would stand idle while you ravaged this world?"

Around me, I sensed a change. Our battered allies stirred,

hope rekindling in their eyes. Even Azhara, magnificent despite her wounds, raised her head with renewed purpose.

But as the demons cowered, retreating from Merlin's light, I couldn't shake a gnawing dread. We'd made a deal with darkness to survive. Would Merlin's judgment fall on us as well?

I turned to Jessica, whispering, "What now? Do we fight... or run?"

I watched, transfixed, as Merlin surveyed the carnage. His eyes, ancient and bottomless as the void, swept across the battlefield. They seemed to pierce through flesh and bone, laying bare the sins of all who stood before him.

My breath caught in my throat. Would he see the darkness that clung to my soul?

Merlin's robes billowed, not with wind, but with barely contained power. Constellations shimmered across the fabric, echoing the cosmic realm from whence he came. In his gnarled hand, he raised a staff that seemed to bend reality around it.

"By the stars," I whispered, unable to tear my gaze away.

Jessica gripped my arm, her nails digging into my flesh. "Michael," she hissed, "we need to—"

But her words were drowned out as Merlin's voice thundered across the battlefield. "Begone, shadows of the abyss!"

The air crackled with energy. I felt it in my bones, a resonance that threatened to tear me apart. Merlin's staff glowed with an otherworldly light, and then—

A wave of pure, cosmic force exploded outward. It washed over me, searing away the taint of dark magic I'd embraced. I screamed, the sound lost in the cacophony of demonic shrieks.

Through tear-filled eyes, I watched as the demons' forms twisted and warped. Their unholy power crumbled like ash in the wind.

"Is this... redemption?" I gasped, falling to my knees. "Or damnation?"

Jessica's laughter, wild and unhinged, was my only answer.

I staggered to my feet, my senses reeling from Merlin's

unleashed power. The battlefield pulsed with a new energy, one that sang of starlight and ancient magic.

"Look!" Jessica cried, pointing to the sky.

Azhara Stormscale, her scales shimmering like polished obsidian, led a squadron of dragons in a breathtaking aerial assault. Their wings beat in perfect synchronicity with Merlin's arcane gestures, as if the conductor and orchestra were one.

"It's beautiful," I whispered, mesmerized by the deadly dance above. "And terrifying."

Lightning crackled between the dragons' jaws, arcing down to incinerate clusters of demons. The air filled with the acrid stench of burning flesh and sulfur.

Jessica grabbed my hand, her touch electric. "We can't just stand here. We have to fight!"

I nodded, summoning what remained of my depleted magical reserves. The spell felt different now, purified somehow by Merlin's presence. "Together, then?"

She smiled a fierce, feral thing. "Always."

We joined the fray, our spells intertwining with the dragons' elemental fury. For the first time since this nightmarish battle began, I felt a flicker of hope.

"They're retreating!" someone shouted.

Indeed, the demonic horde seemed to waver, their earlier confidence shattered. I saw fear in their eyes now – a mirror of the terror they'd inflicted upon us for so long.

"Do you think we can win?" Jessica asked, her voice barely audible above the chaos.

I looked at Merlin, his form radiant with cosmic power, and felt a chill run down my spine. "Yes," I replied. "But at what cost?"

The air thickened, heavy with the weight of two titanic powers about to collide. Merlin stood tall, his staff raised high, a pillar of light against the encroaching darkness. Across from him, the demon lord emerged from the roiling mass of his minions, a creature of nightmare made flesh.

I couldn't breathe. My heart hammered against my ribs, a war drum heralding doom.

"Kael," Jessica whispered, her fingers digging into my arm. "Should we... help?"

I shook my head, words failing me. This was beyond us now. We were insects before giants, leaves caught in a hurricane.

The demon lord's voice boomed across the battlefield, a sound that made my very bones ache. "You dare challenge me, old man?"

Merlin's response was quiet, yet it carried to every ear. "I do not challenge; I end this."

They clashed. Reality itself seemed to buckle and warp around them. Spells of such complexity and power that my mind recoiled from comprehending them tore through the air. The ground beneath our feet groaned and split.

"We should run," I muttered, tugging at Jessica's sleeve. But I couldn't tear my eyes away from the spectacle.

Merlin's face was a mask of concentration, every line etched with determination. The demon lord howled, a sound of fury and... was that fear?

"Look!" Jessica cried out, pointing.

The demon's form was... unraveling. Tendrils of darkness peeled away from its monstrous body, dissipating into nothingness.

Merlin's voice rose in a terrible chant, words that burned my ears and seared themselves into my memory. A vortex of light engulfed the demon lord, and with a final, ear-splitting shriek, it vanished.

Silence fell. A silence so profound it seemed to swallow the world.

I looked at Jessica and saw the same stunned disbelief in her eyes that I felt in my soul.

"Is it... over?" I asked, my voice cracking.

But even as the words left my lips, I knew. The air felt lighter and cleaner. The oppressive weight of evil that had pressed down upon us for so long... was gone.

The silence lingered, heavy and oppressive, as if the very air was hesitant to disturb the fragile peace. I stumbled forward, my legs weak and trembling, surveying the devastation around us. The once-pristine realm now lay in ruins, its ethereal beauty marred by the scars of battle.

"We won," I whispered, the words tasting strange on my tongue. "But at what cost?"

Jessica stood beside me, her face a mask of conflicting emotions. "Michael," she murmured, her voice hoarse from the battle cries that still echoed in my ears. "Look."

I followed her gaze to where Merlin stood, his form silhouetted against the fading chaos. The great wizard seemed smaller, somehow, hunched and weary, the price of victory etched into every line of his ancient face.

"Is this what triumph feels like?" I asked, more to myself than to Jessica. "It's... hollow."

She reached for my hand, her fingers intertwining with mine. The simple gesture grounded me, a reminder of what we'd fought for. "We're alive," she said softly. "That's not nothing."

Around us, the survivors began to stir. Dragons, their scales dulled by exhaustion, limped across the battlefield. Mages slumped against broken pillars, their eyes haunted by the horrors they'd witnessed. The air was thick with the acrid smell of spent magic and spilled blood.

"We should help," Jessica suggested but made no move to leave my side. I nodded, equally reluctant to break this moment of quiet reflection.

In the distance, Azhara Stormscale raised her head, her once-majestic form now battered and torn. Her mournful keen cut through the eerie stillness, a lament for the fallen that chilled me to my core.

"Do you think..." I began, then faltered, unsure how to voice the darkness gnawing at my thoughts. "Do you think we'll ever be the same after this?"

Jessica's grip on my hand tightened. "No," she answered, her honesty as brutal as it was necessary. "But perhaps that's the point."

We stood there amidst the wreckage of our victory, the weight of survival pressing down upon us. The battle was over, but I couldn't shake the feeling that this was merely the eye of the storm. What fresh horrors awaited us in the aftermath of our pyrrhic triumph?

CHAPTER 17

RESOLUTION

The acrid stench of smoke burned my nostrils as I surveyed the carnage around us. Bodies lay strewn across the blood-soaked earth, friend and foe alike rendered equal in death's cold embrace. I caught Michael's eye and saw my own weariness and relief mirrored there. We had won, but at what cost?

"It's over," I murmured, my voice hoarse from battle cries. "We actually did it."

Michael nodded grimly. "For now. But at what price, Jessica?"

His words echoed my own dark thoughts. How many had we sacrificed to achieve this pyrrhic victory? The faces of the fallen flickered through my mind, accusing specters I knew would haunt my dreams.

I turned away, unable to bear the weight of Michael's gaze. My eyes were drawn to Thalia, standing apart from our battered group. She cut an otherworldly figure, silver hair gleaming in the fading light as she stared fixedly at the horizon. Where demonic hordes had poured forth mere hours ago, now only wisps of black mist remained.

Watching her, I felt a chill creep down my spine. There was

something unnerving in her stillness, in the intensity of her violet eyes, as if she saw things beyond mortal ken.

"Thalia?" I called hesitantly. "What do you see?"

She did not turn, did not even blink. When she spoke, her voice held the cadence of prophecy. "The veil between worlds grows thin. They whispered to me about those we had lost. Their spirits linger, restless and unquiet."

A shudder ran through me. How many of those restless dead had fallen by my hand? How many had I failed to save?

"Tell me," I whispered, dreading the answer. "Will their sacrifice be enough? Have we truly won?"

At last, Thalia's gaze shifted to me. The weight of ages lay behind those haunting eyes. "Victory and defeat are never absolute, child. The wheel turns ever onward. Today's triumph may be tomorrow's downfall."

Her cryptic words offered little comfort. As silence fell once more, I turned back to the blood-drenched battlefield. We had won the day, but at what terrible price? And what fresh horrors lay in wait, lurking just beyond the veil of reality?

The silence that descended was heavy as a burial shroud, suffocating in its intensity. I could almost taste the acrid blend of triumph and loss on my tongue, bitter as ashes. Around me, our battered group stood motionless, each lost in their own private hell of memory.

I closed my eyes but found no respite. Behind my lids, faces flickered – comrades who would never again draw breath, their final moments etched in horrifying clarity. My hands trembled, sticky with blood both seen and unseen.

How long we stood thus, I couldn't say. Time seemed to stretch and warp, much as it had in the Ethereal Realm of Dragons. I found myself longing for that place of cosmic beauty, so far removed from this scarred and smoking battlefield.

A shuffling step broke the spell. My eyes snapped open to see Kael Stoneforge moving forward, his usual rakish grin replaced by an expression of grim solemnity. His stormy eyes swept over us, lingering on each face as if committing them to memory.

When he spoke, his voice was low and rough, stripped of its customary humor. "We stand here, victorious," he began, "but victory tastes of ash and regret."

I swallowed hard, fighting back the sob that threatened to escape. Kael's words struck at the very heart of my turmoil.

He continued, "To those who fell – our brothers, our sisters in arms – we owe a debt that can never truly be repaid. Their courage, their sacrifice... it burns brighter than any star in the cosmos."

As he spoke, I found myself wondering about the weight Kael must carry. How many companions had he lost over his long years of magical study and adventure? Did the ghosts of the past haunt his dreams as they did mine?

"May we honor them," Kael's voice grew stronger, "not just with words, but with our actions. Let their memory fuel us in the trials to come."

A murmur of assent rippled through our group. I nodded, even as a chill of foreboding slithered down my spine. What new horrors awaited us on the horizon? And would we have the strength to face them, burdened as we were by grief and exhaustion?

The circle of stones loomed before us, a crude monument to our fallen. Each of us approached in turn, laying tokens upon the rough-hewn altar. I watched, my heart a leaden weight, as Michael placed a tattered page from his spellbook beside a dragon scale left by Eldran.

"For those who taught me," he whispered, his voice cracking.

I knelt before the memorial, my fingers tracing the jagged edges of the stones. The world narrowed to this point of contact – cold, unyielding rock beneath my fingertips. A vortex of memories threatened to pull me under.

"I... I'm sorry," I choked out, my voice barely audible. "I should have been faster, stronger..."

The doubts that had plagued me throughout our journey surged forth. How many times had I hesitated, second-guessed myself? Each moment of indecision now felt like a betrayal.

"Jessica?" Michael's concerned voice cut through my spiraling thoughts.

I looked up, meeting his gaze. "Do you ever wonder if we're truly worthy of their sacrifice?"

He didn't answer immediately, and his brow furrowed in thought. "I don't know," he admitted finally. "But I think... I think they believed we were."

His words hit me like a physical blow. I closed my eyes, remembering the fierce determination I'd seen in our fallen comrades' faces and the unwavering trust they'd placed in us, even as the battle raged at its fiercest.

"We can't let them down," I murmured, more to myself than to Michael.

As I stood, my legs trembling slightly, I felt a change settle over me. The crushing weight of guilt remained, but alongside it, a steely resolve began to take root. We would carry on, not just for ourselves, but for those who could no longer fight.

I placed my hand on the topmost stone, feeling the lingering warmth of the day's sun. "We'll make it count," I vowed softly. "Every moment, every breath. I swear it."

As I turned from the memorial, Michael's hand found mine, his grip firm and reassuring. The weight of our shared experiences hung heavy between us, unspoken yet palpable.

"We've come so far," Michael mused, his voice barely above a whisper. "Remember when it was just us against the world?"

I laughed a brittle sound that surprised even me. "Simpler times. Though I'm not sure, I'd trade our unlikely allies for anything now."

Michael's eyes clouded with memory. "The dwarven smiths of Ironhold, the elven archers... even that cantankerous old wizard."

"Don't forget the dragons," I added, a chill running down my spine at the recollection of their otherworldly beauty and terrible power.

As we spoke, I noticed a subtle shift in the air around us. The oppressive silence that had blanketed our group began to lift, replaced by a low murmur of voices.

"We did it, didn't we?" someone said, their tone a mixture of disbelief and dawning joy.

"Against all odds," another replied, stronger now.

The change was infectious. As if a dam had broken, words of triumph began to flow freely, each voice building upon the last. Even as my heart ached for those we'd lost, I felt a fierce pride blooming in my chest.

We had done the impossible. We had won.

But as the celebrations grew around me, a nagging doubt persisted. What price would we yet pay for this victory? And would I be strong enough to face whatever darkness still lurked on the horizon?

The revelry swelled around me, a cacophony of laughter and tears that seemed to echo the tumultuous emotions churning within my own breast. I found myself recounting the moment when Kael Stoneforge, that gruff mountain of a dwarf, had hurled his mighty war hammer with pinpoint accuracy, felling three demons spawn with a single throw.

"And then," I choked out between hysterical giggles, "he just stood there, stroking his beard, and said, 'Well, that's one way to make an impression.'"

The others roared with laughter, but beneath my mirth, I felt a sharp pang. How many times had Kael's dry humor lifted our spirits in the darkest hours? And now... I pushed the thought away, unwilling to let the specter of grief overtake this fragile moment of joy.

Selene Starfire's ethereal voice cut through the din. "Do you remember when Orin's celestial blade shattered that obsidian monolith? I've never seen such raw power channeled through mortal hands."

I shuddered, recalling the blinding flash and the deafening crack that had followed. The memory of Orin's face at that moment haunted me - a mask of determination barely concealing the agony of wielding such cosmic forces.

As the stories flowed, weaving a tapestry of shared triumph and loss, I felt the bonds between us strengthening, forged anew in the crucible of our shared ordeal. Yet even as warmth blossomed in my chest, a chill crept along my spine. How long would this unity last once the glow of victory faded?

My brooding was interrupted by Eldran Silveroak clearing his throat. The venerable elf's eyes gleamed with an intensity I'd rarely seen as he raised a battered silver chalice.

"Friends," he intoned, his voice carrying the weight of centuries, "let us not forget our most magnificent allies: the dragons, whose celestial flames turned the tide when all seemed lost!"

A chorus of agreement swept through our ragged band. I lifted my own cup, trying to ignore the tremor in my hand. The dragons. Majestic, terrifying, and utterly alien. Their intervention had saved us all, but at what cost? What bargain had we unwittingly struck with those cosmic entities?

As I sipped the bitter wine, I wondered how many of us truly understood the magnitude of what we'd witnessed. And how many, like me, were silently dreading the day when that debt would come due?

The camaraderie slowly ebbed, like a tide retreating to reveal the jagged rocks beneath. Our band dispersed, each drifting away to nurse private wounds and unspoken fears. I found myself drawn to Michael, a moth to his steadying flame.

"Jessica," he murmured, his calloused hand finding mine. "Walk with me?"

I nodded, words trapped behind the lump in my throat. We wandered to the edge of our makeshift camp, the scorched earth crunching beneath our feet. The silence between us stretched taut, filled with the weight of all we'd endured.

"Do you think we're ready?" I finally whispered, my voice raw. "To be... protectors?"

Michael's grip tightened. "I don't know if anyone's ever truly ready for a burden like this."

I laughed, a brittle sound that threatened to shatter. "That's reassuring."

"But we have each other," he continued, his eyes finding mine. "And that's more than most."

I wanted to believe him. Oh, how I yearned for that certainty. But as I gazed at the ravaged landscape, I saw only the echoes of destruction: the price of our victory etched in ash and blood.

"I feel... marked," I confessed, tracing a phantom scar across my heart. "Like we've been branded by this. How do we go back to Earth, to normal, after... after all this?"

Michael's silence was answer enough. There was no going back, only forward, into an uncertain future that loomed like a gathering storm. I closed my eyes, letting the weight of our new reality settle over me like a shroud.

"We carry it with us," I murmured, more to myself than to Michael. "The scars, the memories... they're part of us now, for better or worse."

A cool breeze stirred, carrying the scent of smoke and something else – something ancient and unknowable. A reminder of the cosmic forces we'd brushed against and the terrible responsibility that now rested on our shoulders.

I opened my eyes, meeting Michael's steady gaze. In that moment, I saw my own fears reflected back at me, but also a glimmer of something else. Hope, perhaps. Or at least the determination to forge ahead despite the darkness that threatened to engulf us.

"Together, then," I said, my voice steadier than I felt. "Into whatever comes next."

Michael nodded, a ghost of a smile touching his lips. As we turned back toward camp, I couldn't shake the feeling that we were walking into the maw of something far greater and more terrible than we could possibly imagine. But we would face it side by side, carrying the weight of our hard-won victory and the promise of a new dawn – no matter how bitter it might prove to be.

The others had gathered around the smoldering remnants of our campfire, their faces etched with exhaustion and something deeper – a haunted look I knew all too well. As Michael and I approached, Thalia's eyes met mine, a silent understanding passing between us.

"We've paid a heavy price," Kael rumbled, his voice rough with emotion. "But the bonds forged in battle are not easily broken."

I nodded, my throat tight. "We're more than comrades now. We're... family."

The word hung in the air, fragile and potent. I sensed rather than saw the others straighten, drawing strength from the connection we shared.

"To the family," Eldran said softly, raising an imaginary toast. "And to those who can't be here to share in our victory."

A murmur of agreement rippled through our small circle. As we stood there, bathed in the fading light of day, I felt a shift – subtle, yet undeniable. The weight of our shared experiences settled around us like a cloak, binding us together in ways I couldn't fully comprehend.

"What now?" someone asked – perhaps it was me, my own voice sounding distant and unfamiliar.

Michael's hand found mine, his grip firm and grounding. "We honor their memory," he said, his words carrying the weight of an oath. "By protecting what they died for."

I closed my eyes, feeling the truth of his words resonate within me. When I opened them again, I saw determination mirrored in every face.

"Together," I whispered, the promise echoing in my soul. "We face whatever comes next... together."

As darkness fell, we stood united, guardians of a hard-won peace. The road ahead was shrouded in uncertainty, but at that moment, I knew we'd face it as one – bound by sacrifice, forged in fire, and ready to safeguard the future, no matter the cost.

CHAPTER 18

RETURNING HOME

As I step off the train onto the gritty New York platform, a wave of vertigo washes over me. The city skyline looms, familiar yet alien, as if viewed through a warped lens. Jessica's hand trembles in mine, her eyes wide and unfocused.

"Michael," she whispers, "it doesn't feel real."

I nod, unable to find words. How could I articulate the surreal sensation of returning to a world that no longer feels like home? The echoes of cosmic melodies still resonate in my mind, a haunting reminder of the Ethereal Realm we left behind.

We move through the station, our steps faltering and unsure. The cacophony of the city assaults us - a jarring symphony of car horns, chatter, and the relentless pulse of urban life. Each sound is a tether, pulling us back to a reality we're no longer certain we belong in.

Jessica's grip tightens as we emerge onto the bustling sidewalk. Her eyes dart nervously, scanning faces in the crowd. I know she's searching for signs, for some hint that others can sense the change in us. But they pass by, oblivious to the weight of the cosmic secrets we carry.

We walk in silence, our movements careful and measured. Each step feels like a conscious act of will, as if we're relearning how to exist in this mundane world. The concrete beneath our feet is solid, unyielding - so unlike the ever-shifting landscapes of the Starry Dominion.

A flicker of understanding passes between us as we pause at a crosswalk. Jessica's eyes meet mine, and I see the same mix of fear, wonder, and longing reflected there. We don't need words; our shared journey has forged a connection deeper than language.

"Do you think we'll ever feel normal again?" Jessica asks, her voice barely audible above the city's din.

I consider lying, offering false comfort. But the truth spills out, dark and heavy. "I don't know if we were ever truly normal to begin with."

She nods, a sad smile ghosting across her lips. We continue our slow procession through streets that once felt like home, now as alien as the cosmic pathways we've traversed. The world spins on, unaware of the darkness we've unleashed, the sins that haunt our every step.

The familiar skyline looms before us, a jagged silhouette against the fading day. Each building, each street corner, carries the weight of memories - both old and achingly new. I saw the coffee shop where we used to laugh, be carefree, and be ignorant. Now, it stands as a mocking reminder of innocence lost.

"Michael," Jessica whispers, her voice trembling. "Look."

I follow her gaze to a shop window, its display of a garish array of trinkets and baubles. But it's not the merchandise that has caught her attention; it's our reflections, ghostly and translucent against the glass.

Jessica steps closer, her eyes fixed on her own image. I watch as she reaches out, her fingertips barely grazing the surface. "Is that... really me?"

I want to comfort her, to say something profound. But the words die in my throat because I see it too: the haunted look in our eyes, the way our shoulders hunch as if carrying an invisible burden. We are changed irrevocably.

"I've done terrible things," Jessica murmurs, her voice hollow. "Things I can never take back."

I remember the choices we made in the Ethereal Realm, the compromises, the sacrifices. The line between right and wrong had blurred so easily in that swirling cosmic chaos.

"We did what we had to," I offer, but the words ring hollow even to my own ears.

Jessica turns to me, her eyes brimming with unshed tears. "Did we? Or did we just tell ourselves that to justify our actions?"

I have no answer. We stand there, suspended in a moment of brutal honesty, as the city rushes by around us, oblivious to our inner turmoil.

The park bench calls to me a siren song of familiarity in this city that no longer feels like home. I sink onto its weathered slats, the wood groaning beneath my weight. A weight that feels infinitely heavier than it did mere weeks ago.

Protector. The word echoes in my mind, a mantle I never asked for but now cannot shed. I close my eyes, remembering the swirling galaxies of the Ethereal Realm, the cosmic melodies that still haunt my dreams. What right do I have to guard this mundane world when I can barely guard my own sanity?

"You look like you're carrying the weight of the universe on your shoulders," Jessica's voice cuts through my reverie, a lifeline to reality.

I open my eyes to find her standing before me, her lithe frame silhouetted against the fading sunlight. "Isn't that what we're doing?" I ask, a bitter chuckle escaping my lips.

She sits beside me, our shoulders barely touching. The silence between us is thick with unspoken words, shared memories of terrors and wonders beyond imagining.

"I never wanted this," I whisper, my voice cracking. "To be responsible for... everything."

Jessica's hand finds mine, her grip firm and grounding. "Neither did I," she admits. "But we're in this together now, for better or worse."

I turn to her, searching her face for any hint of doubt. But all I see is the same determination that has always burned in those hazel eyes, tempered now by a wisdom bought at too high a price.

"Together," I echo the words of a promise and a prayer. As we sit there, bathed in the dying light of day, I feel something shift inside me. The burden doesn't lift, but it becomes... bearable. Shared.

The key to our old apartment feels unnaturally heavy in my hand. As I push it into the lock, the mechanism groans in protest as if reluctant to let us back into our former lives. The door swings open with a plaintive creak, revealing a space frozen in time.

We step inside, and the scent of dust and neglect assaults my nostrils. It's a stark reminder of how long we've been gone and how much we've changed.

"God, it's like walking into a tomb," Jessica mutters, her voice barely above a whisper.

I nod, unable to form words as we move through the rooms. Each object, each piece of furniture, seems to mock us with memories of a simpler existence. The coffee mug I left on the kitchen counter is now home to a family of dead insects. The unfinished novel on the nightstand, its pages yellowed and brittle.

Jessica pauses by the bookshelf, her fingers tracing the spines of long-forgotten volumes. "Do you remember when our biggest worry was paying the rent?" she asks, a hollow laugh escaping her lips.

I'm about to respond when something catches her eye. She reaches for a small frame hidden behind a stack of magazines. As she pulled it out, I saw her body stiffen.

"Jess?" I approach cautiously, peering over her shoulder.

In her hands is a photograph of us, taken on our first date. We're laughing, carefree, oblivious to the fate that awaited us. Jessica's hands tremble as she stares at our past selves.

"We were so... innocent," she whispers, her voice thick with emotion. "How can we ever go back to that? How can we pretend to be normal after everything we've seen, everything we've done?"

I watch as tears begin to form in her eyes, and I feel my own throat tighten. "I don't know if we can," I admit, the words tasting like ash in my mouth.

I place my hand on Jessica's shoulder, feeling the weight of our shared burdens. "But maybe we're not meant to go back," I say softly, my voice barely above a whisper. "We've changed, Jess. We've grown."

She turns to me, her eyes searching mine. I see the pain there but also a flicker of something else. Hope, perhaps. Or resignation.

"We've made mistakes," I continue, the words coming unbidden. "God knows we've both done things we regret. But we've learned from them. We're stronger now. Wiser."

Jessica nods slowly, her gaze drifting back to the photograph. "But at what cost?" she murmurs.

I take a deep breath, feeling the weight of our experiences pressing down on me. "The cost was high," I admit. "But we're still here. We're still fighting."

A silence falls between us, heavy with unspoken thoughts. Then, unexpectedly, a memory surfaces.

"Remember that time in the Ethereal Realm," I begin, a hint of amusement creeping into my voice, "when Kael tried to impress Azhara with his 'mastery' of Dragon lore?"

Jessica's lips twitch, a ghost of a smile. "And he accidentally insulted her entire lineage?"

"I thought she was going to incinerate him on the spot," I chuckle, the sound strange in the stillness of our old apartment.

Jessica's laugh, when it comes, is rusty but genuine. "His face when she started reciting *his* family history..."

For a moment, we're transported back to that surreal moment, surrounded by swirling galaxies and the scent of stardust. The laughter fades, but something of that otherworldly magic lingers, a reminder of the incredible journey we've shared.

"We've seen wonders," I murmur, meeting Jessica's gaze. "And horrors. But we've faced them together."

She nods, her fingers intertwining with mine. "Together," she echoes, and I feel the strength of her resolve.

I lead Jessica up the creaking stairs to the rooftop, each step echoing with memories of a lifelong past. We emerge into the fading light, the city sprawling before us like a concrete jungle bathed in crimson and gold.

"It's beautiful," Jessica whispers, her voice barely audible above the distant hum of traffic.

I nod, unable to shake the feeling that we're trespassers in our own world. The setting sun casts long shadows across the rooftops, transforming familiar landmarks into ominous silhouettes. In the deepening twilight, I can almost see the tendrils of darkness that once threatened to consume us all.

"Do you think they're watching?" Jessica asks, her gaze fixed on the horizon. "Althea and the others?"

I swallow hard, remembering the High Priestess's radiant face, her eyes shimmering with an otherworldly light. "I hope so," I murmur. "I hope they know their sacrifice wasn't in vain."

Jessica's hand finds mine, her grip tight. "I keep seeing Kael's face," she confesses, her voice breaking. "The moment he... when he..."

I pull her close, feeling her body tremble against mine. "I know," I whisper, my own throat constricting. "I see it, too, every time I close my eyes."

We stand in silence, the weight of our losses pressing down upon us. The city below continues its ceaseless rhythm, oblivious to the cosmic battle that nearly tore reality apart. How many of these people, I wonder, will ever know how close they came to oblivion?

"Do you think we made the right choice?" Jessica asks, her words barely a breath.

I hesitate, memories of the Ethereal Realm flooding my mind

– the swirling galaxies, the cosmic melodies, the raw power that coursed through our veins. "We did what we had to," I reply, but the words ring hollow in my ears.

As darkness descends, I can't shake the feeling that our greatest trials still lie ahead. The shadows lengthen, and with them, the whispers of doubt that have plagued me since our return. What price will we ultimately pay for our victory?

I turn away from the skyline, my heart heavy with the weight of our newfound responsibility. Jessica's eyes meet mine, a silent understanding passing between us. We've changed irrevocably so.

"It's time," I say, my voice low and gravelly.

Jessica nods, her shoulders squaring. "We can't run from this, can we?"

"No," I admit, taking her hand. "But we face it together."

We descend the stairs, each step echoing with finality. The hallway stretches before us, familiar yet alien. I can't shake the feeling that unseen eyes watch our every move, judging and waiting.

At our apartment door, Jessica pauses. "Michael," she whispers, "do you ever wonder if we're still... us?"

I swallow hard, memories of star fire and dragon scales flashing behind my eyes. "I don't know," I confess. "But whoever we are now, it's who we need to be."

The key turns in the lock, and a sound that once meant safety is now loaded with foreboding. As the door swings open, I catch a glimpse of our reflection in the hallway mirror – two figures, battle-worn and haunted, yet standing tall.

"Ready?" I ask, though I'm not sure I am myself.

Jessica's grip tightens on my hand. "As we'll ever be."

We step inside, the door closing behind us with a soft click that feels more like the sealing of a tomb. In the darkness of our apartment, I can almost hear the whispers of cosmic forces reminding us of the oath we've taken.

Guardians of Earth. The title sits uneasily on my shoulders, a mantle I'm not sure I deserve. But as Jessica flicks on the light, I see a glimmer of hope in her eyes that steadies my resolve.

Whatever comes next, we'll face it together.

CHAPTER 19

EPILOGUE

Cunning but unreliable narrator. Past tense. Gothic and melancholic. Sparse description. Haunting language with a rhythmic cadence. Focus on psychological torment. Subtle, creeping horror. Characters haunted by past sins. Dark, atmospheric settings that evoke dread. Varied pacing. Heightened tension.

I stood atop the hill, my eyes tracing the horizon where dragons once soared. The landscape stretched before us, serene yet eerily empty. Michael's presence beside me was a cold comfort.

"They're truly gone," I whispered, my voice hollow.

"Yes," Michael replied, his tone flat. "But at what cost?"

I couldn't answer. The weight of our actions, of the choices we'd made, pressed down upon me like a shroud. The dragons had departed, leaving behind a world both saved and irreparably changed. Their absence gnawed at me, a persistent ache in the pit of my stomach.

We descended the hill in silence, each lost in our own thoughts. The path to the chamber seemed to twist and writhe beneath our feet as if the very earth rejected our presence. I wondered, not for the first time, whether we had made the right choice.

The chamber awaited us, dim and suffocating. Candlelight flickered, casting long shadows that danced across the walls like restless spirits. Our allies gathered around a table, and their faces grave in the wavering light.

High Priestess Althea's voice broke the silence, gentle yet resonant. "We have achieved peace, but at what price?"

I couldn't meet her gaze, afraid of the judgment I might find there. Instead, I focused on the candle flames, their dance hypnotic and accusatory.

"The dragons entrusted us with this world's protection," Selene Starfire interjected, her eyes swirling with cosmic depths. "We must honor their sacrifice."

Sacrifice. The word echoed in my mind, a relentless refrain. How much had we sacrificed to reach this point? How much blood stained our hands?

"We forged this path," Orin Emberforge rumbled, his voice like distant thunder. "Now we must walk it, no matter how treacherous."

I nodded, though doubt gnawed at me. The chamber seemed to close in, the air thick with unspoken fears and lingering regrets. Our newfound peace felt fragile, a delicate illusion that might shatter at any moment.

As discussions of responsibility and vigilance filled the air, I retreated into my thoughts. The dragons' departure replayed in my mind, their majestic forms fading into the Ethereal Realm. Had we truly saved the world or merely postponed its doom?

The candlelight flickered, and for a moment, I thought I saw accusing eyes in the shadows. The weight of our choices, of the lives lost and the bonds broken, threatened to crush me. Peace, it seemed, came at a terrible price—one we might be paying for eternity.

A hush fell over the chamber as Merlin stepped forward, his presence commanding even in the dim light. His robes shimmered with an otherworldly iridescence as if woven from the very fabric of twilight. When he spoke, his voice resonated with the weight of eons.

"Children of Earth," he intoned, each word a caress and a warning, "you stand at the precipice of a new era. The dragons have departed, but their legacy endures through you."

I shivered, feeling the truth of his words seep into my bones. My gaze flickered to the shadows, half-expecting to see accusatory specters lurking there. But only the flickering candlelight greeted me, casting long, dancing shadows across the stone walls.

Merlin's eyes, ancient and knowing, seemed to pierce through my soul. "Jessica," he said, my name a gentle command. "Your journey has been fraught with peril and pain. Yet here you stand, a guardian of this realm."

My throat constricted as memories flooded my mind—the ordinary life I'd left behind, the crucible of fire and magic that had forged me anew. "I'm not worthy," I whispered, the words escaping before I could stop them.

A sad smile played at the corners of Merlin's lips. "None of us are truly worthy," he replied, his voice a soothing balm. "It is in striving that we find our purpose."

I closed my eyes, allowing his wisdom to wash over me. The weight of my past mistakes pressed down, a constant, aching reminder. How many had suffered because of my choices? How many souls cried out from beyond the veil, demanding justice I could never provide?

"The path of a protector is never easy," Merlin continued, addressing the group but seeming to speak directly to my burdened heart. "You will face darkness, both without and within. But remember, it is in confronting our shadows that we find our true strength."

I opened my eyes, meeting Merlin's gaze. In those fathomless orbs, I saw reflected the vastness of the Ethereal Realm—a reminder of the cosmic forces we now stood against. A chill ran down my spine, a premonition of trials yet to come.

"I accept this burden," I said, my voice barely above a whisper. "Whatever the cost."

Michael's hand found mine in the dim light, his touch grounding me in the present. I turned to him, searching his face for any trace of the uncertainty that had once plagued us both. Instead, I found a resolute calm that both awed and unsettled me.

"We've come so far," he said, his voice carrying a newfound strength. "The dragons... they showed us what we're capable of. What we must become."

A murmur of agreement rippled through the gathering. I watched as Michael stood, his silhouette cast long and spectral against the flickering candlelight.

"Merlin," he continued, addressing our enigmatic mentor, "your teachings, the legacy of the dragons – they're not just lessons. They're a sacred trust."

I felt a swell of pride, tinged with a familiar dread. How much more would be asked of us? How much more could we bear?

"We must remain vigilant," a voice from the shadows intoned. I recognized it as Lyra's, her words laden with the weight of her own haunted past. "The world teeters on a knife's edge, and we are its guardians."

"United," another voice added. Marcus, I realized, was his usual bravado tempered by the gravity of our circumstances.

I closed my eyes, allowing their words to wash over me. We were bound now, forged in the crucible of cosmic conflict. But at what cost? What pieces of ourselves had we left behind in the Ethereal Realm?

"Together," I whispered, more to myself than to the others. "We stand together, or we fall alone."

The silence that followed was heavy with unspoken fears and shared resolve. At that moment, I felt the true weight of our new reality pressing down upon us all.

As the meeting drew to a close, Merlin rose, his twilight robes shimmering with an otherworldly light. His eyes, ancient and piercing, swept across our faces.

"Remember," he intoned, his voice carrying the weight of eons, "light and darkness are but two sides of the same coin. One cannot exist without the other."

A chill ran down my spine as Merlin's words hung in the air, thick and oppressive. The candles flickered, casting monstrous shadows on the walls.

"The balance is fragile," he continued, "and chaos... chaos is always waiting."

I shuddered, my mind reeling with visions of the horrors we'd faced. Would they ever truly be vanquished?

As we filed out of the chamber, Michael's hand found mine in the darkness. "Let's walk," he whispered.

The garden path stretched before us, bathed in silvery moonlight. Each step crunched softly under our feet, a rhythmic counterpoint to the eerie silence.

"Jessica," Michael began, his voice barely above a whisper, "do you ever wonder if we're truly ready for this?"

I laughed, a hollow sound that echoed in the still night air. "Ready? I'm not sure I even know what that means anymore."

We paused beside a gnarled old tree, its branches reaching toward the star-studded sky like grasping fingers.

"I fear," I admitted, the words clawing their way out of my throat, "that we've only seen the beginning, that there are darker days ahead."

Michael's grip on my hand tightened. "We've come so far," he said, but I could hear the doubt lurking beneath his words.

I turned to face him, searching his eyes for a glimmer of the carefree man I once knew. But I saw only my own haunted reflection staring back.

My gaze drifted upward, tracing constellations I'd never noticed before. Somewhere beyond those twinkling points of light, the dragons soared through the Ethereal Realm. A realm I could scarcely imagine, yet one that had changed everything.

"Do you think they can see us?" I murmured, my voice catching. "The dragons, I mean. From their cosmic sanctuary."

Michael remained silent; his presence was a steady anchor beside me.

"We owe them everything," I continued, my chest tightening with an overwhelming surge of gratitude. "This peace... it's because of them. Because they chose to intervene when all seemed lost."

I closed my eyes, remembering the awe-inspiring sight of Azhara Stormscale's true form, her scales gleaming like polished obsidian as she led the charge against our foes. The memory burned, bright and terrible.

"Sometimes," I confessed, "I wake up convinced it was all a dream, that we're still fighting, still losing."

Michael's hand settled on my shoulder, warm and reassuring. I leaned into his touch, desperate for something solid to cling to.

"We're not dreaming, Jessica," he said softly. "And we're not alone."

I turned to face him, searching his stormy eyes. "How can you be so sure?"

"Because," he replied, a hint of his old mischief flickering across his face, "Kael would never let us hear the end of it if we gave up now."

A laugh bubbled up from somewhere deep inside me, surprising us both. It felt strange, almost foreign, after so much darkness.

"You're right," I admitted. "We have a duty now: to Earth, to each other, to our allies."

Michael nodded solemnly. "Together," he said, "we'll face whatever comes next."

As we stood there, bathed in starlight, I felt a fragile hope begin to take root. But beneath it, a nagging whisper persisted: What price would we ultimately pay for this hard-won peace?

As if sensing my unease, a playful breeze swept through the garden, rustling the leaves around us. It carried with it the scent of night-blooming jasmine, sweet and intoxicating. The wind tugged at my hair, tousling it into wild disarray.

I couldn't help but laugh again, the sound startling in its genuineness. "The spirits are feeling mischievous tonight," I remarked, a wry smile tugging at my lips.

Michael's eyes crinkled with amusement. "Or perhaps they're reminding us that there's still joy to be found in this world we've sworn to protect."

For a moment, we were just two people in a moonlit garden, unburdened by the weight of cosmic responsibility. It was a fleeting reprieve but one I clung to desperately.

"We should head back," I said reluctantly, the moment slipping away like sand through an hourglass. "The others will be waiting."

As we made our way back to the chamber, a somber mood descended once more. The hallways seemed to whisper with the echoes of ancient battles and forgotten sacrifices. Each step felt heavier than the last.

We entered the room to find our allies gathered in solemn silence. High Priestess Althea's golden hair gleamed in the candlelight, her serene expression a stark contrast to the tension that crackled in the air.

"My friends," she intoned, her voice as melodious as ever, "our vigil begins anew."

One by one, our companions nodded their assent and took their leave. The weight of our shared duty hung heavy in the air, a palpable thing. As I watched them go, I couldn't shake the feeling that we were all teetering on the edge of a precipice, staring into an abyss of untold challenges.

Yet beneath the dread that coiled in my stomach, a flicker of determination burned. We had overcome impossible odds before. Whatever darkness lay ahead, we would face it together.

As the last of our allies departed, Michael turned to me, his blue eyes reflecting the dying embers of the hearth. "Shall we?" he asked, gesturing toward the eastern balcony.

I nodded, my throat tight with unspoken emotions. We made our way through the winding corridors, the stone walls seeming to close in around us with each step. The air grew thick with the scent of impending dawn, a mixture of dew and possibility that set my nerves on edge.

We emerged onto the balcony just as the first rays of sunlight began to pierce the veil of night. The world before us was achingly familiar yet irrevocably changed. Rolling hills stretched out to the horizon, their verdant slopes unmarred by the scars of recent battles. But the absence of dragons wheeling through the sky left an emptiness that gnawed at my soul.

"It's beautiful," Michael murmured, his voice rough with emotion. "And terrifying."

I leaned into him, drawing strength from his solid presence. "We've come so far," I whispered, memories of our harrowing journey flashing through my mind like shards of broken glass. "But the road ahead..."

"We'll face it together," he said firmly, his hand finding mine in the growing light.

As the sun climbed higher, bathing us in its golden glow, I felt a curious mixture of gratitude and resolve wash over me. We had lost so much and sacrificed more than I ever thought possible. Yet here we stood, on the threshold of a new dawn, guardians of a world reborn.

"We're not alone," I said, more to myself than to Michael. "Whatever comes next, we have each other. We have our allies."

But even as the words left my lips, a chill ran down my spine. For in the shadows that still clung to the corners of the balcony, I sensed the lingering presence of past sins and future trials. Our vigil had only just begun.

A whisper of wind rustled through my hair, carrying with it the faintest scent of ozone and ancient magic. My gaze was drawn to the distant horizon, where reality seemed to shimmer and blur.

"Do you feel that?" I breathed, my heart quickening.

Michael nodded, his eyes narrowing. "Merlin," he said softly.

Though the great warlock was nowhere to be seen, his presence lingered like a half-remembered dream. I closed my eyes, allowing the sensation to wash over me. At that moment, I could almost hear his voice, rich with centuries of wisdom, echoing in the chambers of my mind.

"We carry his legacy now," I murmured, a weight settling on my shoulders. "All that he taught us, all that he sacrificed..."

"It's a heavy burden," Michael agreed, his voice tight with emotion.

I opened my eyes, meeting his gaze. "But we're not alone in bearing it," I reminded him, thinking of our allies, scattered across the world but united in purpose.

As we stood there, bathed in the light of a new day, I felt a surge of courage coursing through my veins. Merlin's teachings, his unwavering belief in the power of unity and courage in the face of darkness, had become a part of us.

"We won't let him down," I vowed, my voice barely above a whisper. "Whatever comes, we'll face it together."

The wind picked up again, and for a moment, I could have sworn I heard the faintest echo of Merlin's laughter in the breeze. A reminder that even in his absence, his watchful eye remained upon us, guiding and inspiring from beyond the veil of this world.

www.ingramcontent.com/pod-product-compliance
Lightning Source LLC
Chambersburg PA
CBHW070900160726

48004CB00003B/1178